Mirror, Mirror

Come into the world of
MIRROR, MIRROR, where each
story is a reflection of what is real and
what is magic. What at first seem like
familiar folk or fairy tales dramatically
transform into strange and new stories of
horror and temptation. Will you sniff the
forbidden flowers, can you crawl behind
the looking glass, can your parents tear
you apart and what's the terrible
secret of the conjuror's trick?
Can you see yourself in the
MIRROR, MIRROR?

First published in Great Britain in 2002 by
The Chicken House
2 Palmer Street, Frome,
Somerset BA11 1DS, United Kingdom
E-mail: chickenhouse@doublecluck.com

ISBN 1 903434 50 5

British Library Cataloguing in Publication data available.

Cover illustration by David Wyatt
Cover design by Alison Withey

Typeset in Great Britain by Dorchester Typesetting Group Ltd
Printed and bound in Great Britain by Cox & Wyman Ltd

Mirror, Mirror

Silverman

The Chicken House

2 Palmer Street, Frome
Somerset BA11 1DS

Mirror, Mirror

A child in the mirror sees a hero,
a hero in the mirror sees a gambler,
a gambler in the mirror sees a bride.

A bride in the mirror sees a captive,
a captive in the mirror sees a soldier,
a soldier in the mirror sees a coward.

A coward in the mirror sees a rebel,
a rebel in the mirror sees an outcast,
an outcast in the mirror sees a beast.

A beast in the mirror sees a child.

Contents

Dying for Franjibelle

Yolande was older than her sister by two years. She loved her sister Camilla dearly and her sister loved her. They shared the same bedroom and in the solitude of night, when the rest of the household were drenched in sleep, they pledged to each other that their love would last forever and that whenever one of them was in need, the other would come to her assistance.

One Saturday afternoon they were on their way to the burger bar, where they had arranged to meet some friends. Strolling over the iron-railed bridge, they heard a boy calling to them.

"Hi there!"

"Oh no!" Camilla said. "It's Neil."

Neil wasn't one of their friends. There was something scary about him – the way he could be nasty to other kids or hurt them, and the way he swore about teachers behind their backs. And his eyes always looked wild, as if he were hunting for ways to cause trouble.

"Hello Neil," Yolande said. "We can't stop long. We're meeting friends in town at two o'clock."

"No problem," Neil said. "I just thought you might like to see something down there."

He pointed towards the riverbank.

"What is it?" Yolande asked.

"Ever heard of franjibelle?"

"Never. What's that?"

"You won't believe your eyes," he said. "It's a flower that blooms only once every seven years. It has violet and red petals and it's huge." With his hands he formed a circle larger than a dinner plate.

"Wow!" Yolande exclaimed. "Is it in flower now?"

"Yes."

"We can't come now, we'll be late," Camilla urged her sister.

"Okay," Yolande agreed. "Perhaps another time, Neil."

"There's no other time!" Neil said. "Unless you mean in seven years … "

Yolande took Camilla's hand.

"Come on," she said. "Let's go look. It won't take long."

They followed Neil down under the bridge then alongside the broad, murky river. They walked for several minutes, until the old shipyard came into view, with its rusting cranes and abandoned warehouses.

"I thought it was just down here on the river-bank," Camilla said.

"It is," Neil answered. "Just a bit further."

They walked on until they reached a small cluster of trees. Neil turned off the path and crawled under a fence, then held up the barbed wire so that Yolande and Camilla could climb through.

Under the trees it was much darker. As their eyes adjusted, Yolande and Camilla beheld a circle of young people sitting around on logs. They all seemed lost in their own thoughts.

"There it is," Neil said, pointing to a plant growing within the circle.

Yolande and Camilla approached the plant. It certainly was weird. The outermost rims of the huge petals were dark violet and their texture was velvety. Towards the centre, where the petals joined, the violet merged to lilac and was flecked with red, as if someone had spilled drops of blood on it.

"Why don't you smell it?" Neil suggested. But before they could respond, they heard a voice chanting:

"One sniff and you're in heaven,
Two and you're in hell,
Three, leave the world forever
Dying for franjibelle."

The voice came from a dreamy girl who was sitting on a log watching the sisters.

"Come on, let's go!" urged Camilla once more.

"One sniff will be alright," Neil said. "Look! I'll do it."

He bent over the franjibelle and placed his nose near the centre of the violet flower. Then he inhaled its powerful scent. Almost immediately a smile spread over his face, as if he were experiencing a delicious pleasure.

Without hesitating, Yolande did the same. Oh, how luscious that scent was as it rushed into her lungs – never before had she felt anything so tingly!

"Camilla, it's gorgeous!" she gasped. "You must try it!"

Camilla finally yielded and bent over the flower to inhale its marvellous aroma.

"See," Yolande said. "It's beautiful, isn't it?"

Neil led them over to one of the logs so that they could sit. He squatted down beside them.

Yolande threw back her head and laughed. She felt deliriously happy. She gazed up through the leaves and observed the sunlight streaming down. It fascinated her that she could actually see sunbeams. Millions of them. And each sunbeam was constructed from minute rectangles, each of which reflected rainbow colours. She saw the sunbeams bouncing off leaves, just like rain bouncing off a hard surface. She noticed how the leaves themselves were breathing. They were taking in great gulps of air, feeding the air to the branches and trunk of the great trees. In so doing, they were making themselves green. Oh, it was all quite magical, with butterflies fluttering around weightlessly in the air.

When she turned to look at Camilla, she couldn't believe how exquisite she was! Like an angel, with her large black eyes. And even Neil — how sweet and innocent he looked! What a cheeky smile he gave her, as if to say, "Aren't you glad I brought you down here?" Then she caught sight of her own arms, with those soft hairs growing in precise patterns. "What a strange creature I am," she thought. She took off her shoes and socks, admiring her ten peculiar toes, then stood up and began to twirl around, moving from person to person, peering into their eyes and laughing. The girl who had chanted the franjibelle verse joined her dance. They held hands and swung each other round, laughing and shrieking with joy. Yolande didn't even know this stranger's name, but already she loved her like a sister.

The girl, parting from Yolande, approached the franjibelle again and bent over for a sniff. Yolande followed her. How mysterious the franjibelle now seemed! Like a magic fountain springing from the earth to bring delight to all who came under its spell. It was the source of all happiness. She bent over.

"No, Yolande!"

It was Camilla. She had run over to prevent her sister taking a second sniff. But she was too late! Already, the intoxicating aroma had entered Yolande's nose and lungs.

"One sniff and you're in heaven,
Two and you're in hell,
Three, leave the world forever
Dying for franjibelle."

The girl who had danced with Yolande was chanting again, swirling herself around. This time Yolande didn't join her. A profound nausea had taken hold of her and, as if the weather had suddenly changed, she began hugging herself to keep warm. Everything before her eyes now appeared horrific. The trees were giant ogres with gnarled trunks and vicious arms grabbing at the air. And why were there so many horrid little bats flying around? Neil looked unmistakably evil. "What is he up to?" she wondered. And what about her own sister Camilla – why was she so angry? Yolande had never seen her like that before, with her eyes so cruel, her mouth so snarling and deceptive! Was Camilla a demon? Why had Yolande never noticed this wickedness in her own sister before?

Suddenly, her thoughts were interrupted by a pandemonium of screams and yells. A gang of men, shouting and wielding sticks, were invading the secret hide-out of the franjibelle sniffers. They rushed around the circle, grabbing some of the boys and girls and tying them with ropes. A few managed to escape, running for their lives along the riverbank. Yolande was seized by a brutish man with an unshaven face who bound her hands and legs. For a moment Camilla had the chance to escape! There was a clear way out if she ran for it. But when she saw Yolande being captured, she hesitated, and in that instant she too was overpowered. An enormous fellow, wearing a black scarf wrapped around his head so that nothing showed but his eyes, took hold of her and tied her up.

While Camilla was being bound, she noticed that Neil had not been captured. Instead of trying to escape, he waited until one of the men passed him a bundle of money which he pocketed. "We'll come for more next week," the unshaven man said.

The captives, seven in all, five girls and two boys, were marched down a path leading away from the shipyard until they reached two vans parked on a gravel road. The men bundled the captives inside, climbed into the front seats, then drove off at high speed.

Yolande and Camilla were together in one van, bound fast, but this gave them no comfort. Suddenly Camilla rolled over to Yolande and bit her arm. "It's all your fault!" she cried. "We should never have gone with Neil, we should never have sniffed that evil flower, it's all your fault!"

The van travelled for hours and hours. The captives were given neither food nor water. Night came and still the van sped on and on. By dawn, it was apparent that they were travelling through a mountainous region, because the van was struggling up steep hills.

Eventually, after a day and half of non-stop driving, the van came to a halt. The back doors were flung open.

"Get out, all of you!" the unshaven man barked.

It was difficult for the captives to move with their arms and legs bound. They were also weak from lack of nourishment and from being cooped up in the back of the rattling van for so long. Despite that, the man roughly forced them to stand in a row.

Camilla looked around and saw an enormous mansion, set amidst lawns and ornamental gardens. The front door opened and a man wearing dark glasses and a black leather jacket strode out to meet them.

Solemnly, he greeted the unshaven man and inspected the row of captives. He stopped at Yolande, forced open her mouth and examined her teeth.

"She'll do," the owner of the mansion said. "And these three." He nodded towards Camilla and the two boys.

Then he handed a wedge of banknotes to the unshaven man, who said, "Thank you, Mr Axel."

The three remaining captives were herded back into the van. It set off down the driveway towards the huge wrought iron gates, which opened automatically, allowing it to leave the property.

Yolande, Camilla and the two boys were left alone with Mr Axel.

"You all work for me now!" he bellowed. "From now on, you will obey my every command! Is that understood?"

He pulled a long, curved knife out from his belt. Yolande was petrified! What if she were to be murdered here in this unknown place?

Mr Axel approached the captives. But instead of injuring them, he cut the ropes which bound their hands and feet.

"There is no way out," he explained. "The perimeter walls, as you can see, are extremely high. The gates are controlled by my security guards. They have orders to never let any of you out into the world again. So you had better get used to it here. I expect total loyalty and hard work from each of you. In return, you will be housed and fed."

The captives were shown to their quarters: one dingy room for the two sisters and another for the boys. Although there were no beds, just a skimpy mattress on the stone floor, Yolande and Camilla were so tired they fell asleep immediately.

Their lives at the Axel mansion were miserable. A daily slog of cooking, serving, fetching and cleaning with never so much as a single word of kindness or thanks from Mr Axel. On the contrary, they were often punished for the most trivial mistakes, confined alone in a dark basement room without food for days.

How many years they spent slaving at Mr Axel's mansion they never knew. All the time that they were there, the sisters were never a comfort to each other, and that was the most intense pain of all. Every minute of every day, Camilla burned with rage and bitterness, blaming Yolande for what had befallen them. In time, they grew to hate each other as much as they had once loved each other.

Every month, Mr Axel hosted an extravagant party. These parties were a terrible ordeal for the servants. Gargantuan feasts had to be prepared for

guests who arrived wearing bird and animal costumes to eat and drink and dance through the night,
before driving off at dawn in their swanky cars.
Whole pigs were roasted on spits and the long
tables were laden with every sort of exotic food
imaginable. Countless barrels of liquor were consumed. The servants worked all night, cooking,
serving, fetching and cleaning, until their feet and
hands were blistered with weariness. But they were
never permitted to sleep until the mess which had
been left after the banquet was cleared away.

During one particularly riotous party, Mr Axel
provided his guests with a treat which Yolande and
Camilla immediately recognised. He placed a large
flower with velvety violet petals in the centre of a
round table. It was frangibelle!

The guests approached the flower and after the
first sniff were soon mesmerised by its effects.
They laughed ecstatically, skipping and dancing
around the ornamental gardens. After the second
sniff, fierce arguments and scuffles broke out
between the costumed guests. They threatened
each other, swearing and cursing violently. After the
third sniff, they began to feel faint, and were soon
vomiting, stumbling and falling to the ground in
profound unconsciousness.

By the time dawn broke, Mr Axel and all his
guests were laid out like corpses exactly where they
had fallen. It was eerie and silent, like a battlefield
after a dreadful slaughter.

Yolande, seeing an opportunity to get some shut-eye before the great clean up, sneaked off to her room. But she hadn't been asleep long when Camilla came barging in.

"Now's our chance!" she said.

"What?" Yolande asked irritably, for she was very fatigued. She thought Camilla was so spiteful to wake her from her sleep.

"We must get out of here!"

"I'm too tired to go anywhere," Yolande groaned. "I've been working all night. I'm exhausted. Let me sleep."

"Yolande! Camilla called out. "Yolande! Don't close your eyes! Wake up!"

She shook her sister roughly, trying to rouse her. "Yolande!" Camilla shouted, lifting her sister into a sitting position. "Let's get out of here!"

Yolande rubbed her tired eyes. Eventually she opened them and looked around. Where was she? And who were all these boys and girls slumbering dreamily around her? They were all sprawled out on logs in a circle under a cluster of trees. She recognised one of the boys – it was Neil. In the middle of the circle, she saw a weird flower. It was larger than a dinner plate with violet petals flecked with red.

Camilla was talking to her.

"You shouldn't have sniffed the franjibelle twice! Come on, we have to go now. Our friends are waiting for us at the burger bar, remember? We have to meet them at two o'clock!"

"What's the time now?"

"Quarter to," Camilla answered. "Come on, if we hurry we can just make it." She helped Yolande put on her shoes, then lifted her to her feet.

"You're not going already, are you?" Neil asked. "What about another sniff of franjibelle?"

"No thank you," Camilla said. "We have to go now."

Camilla supported Yolande as they left the circle of people and staggered back through the trees to the riverbank.

A chanting voice floated after them:
"One sniff and you're in heaven,
Two and you're in hell,
Three, leave the world forever
Dying for franjibelle."

Tug of War

Cynthia lived in a faraway city inhabited by people like you and me but with different names and faces. Both her mother and father loved her very much. She had her own room in the house, with pictures from her favourite films on the walls.

They lived happily, all three together. Her mother helped her to make a patchwork quilt and her father built her a tree-house. She loved her mother and father as much as they loved her. Sometimes, they took her on a picnic or went to the cinema with her. It was all great fun.

But there came a time when Cynthia's father and mother began to argue and squabble. Night after night they called each other all the names under the sun.

"You great oaf!" Cynthia's mother called her father. "You can't just have your own way all the time!"

"Who are you to complain?" Cynthia's father replied. "You are never nice to me any more, you stupid cow!"

"How dare you call me that!" Cynthia's mother shouted. "You dumb clod of earth!"

"You should speak, you old bag!" Cynthia's father retorted.

And so it went on, night after night, week after week, month after month and year after year. These squabbles always ended with her mother crying and her father marching out of the house, slamming the front door and not coming back for hours. It made Cynthia unhappy to realise that they were no longer fond of each other. She hated hearing their arguments.

In the end, Cynthia's father and mother decided to live in separate houses.

"But only on one condition," Cynthia's mother said.

"And what's that?" Cynthia's father asked.

"That Cynthia stays with me."

Cynthia's father's face turned red as it swelled with rage.

"No way! She goes with me."

"But I can give her more love!" Cynthia's mother insisted. "A girl needs her mother."

"That's not true, you selfish bitch!" Cynthia's father yelled. "I can give her just as much love, and a girl needs her father."

"You lying scoundrel!" Cynthia's mother fumed. "I love her more and she stays with me. You wouldn't even know how to look after her."

And with that she grabbed hold of Cynthia's left arm and pulled it towards her.

Immediately, Cynthia's father grabbed hold of her right arm and pulled as hard as he could.

"I love her more," he shouted. "You can't even afford to keep her."

Cynthia's father and mother pulled and pulled, but neither was able to pull Cynthia out of the other's grasp.

Cynthia, as you can imagine, wasn't enjoying all this. It was beginning to hurt a lot!

"You're only doing this to get at me!" Cynthia's mother bawled, and she pulled twice as hard as she'd been pulling before.

"You only want to punish me!" Cynthia's father responded, and he pulled twice as hard as he'd been pulling before.

At that moment, Cynthia's grandad came in from the back garden.

"He's stealing my Cynthia!" her mother yelled.

At first, Grandad was confused. But when he understood what was going on, he hobbled over to help Cynthia's mother.

"That's not fair!" Cynthia's father exclaimed.

The front door opened and in walked Uncle Sid, who was coming to visit.

"Help me, Sid!" Cynthia's father bellowed. "She belongs with me!"

Sid rushed in and took the side of Cynthia's father.

"I love her more!" Cynthia's mother shouted. "Let go!"

"I love her more!" Cynthia's father yelled. "You let go!"

If only they would have noticed how much all this was hurting Cynthia, they might have stopped. Tears of pain were streaming from her eyes.

But no! On the contrary, they all pulled and yanked and tugged and heaved. And they made such an awful noise, the neighbours heard and came running in.

Mr Sprig, the left-hand neighbour, joined Cynthia's mother's side, and Mrs Dewar, the right-hand neighbour, joined Cynthia's father's side.

"She's staying with me, you vile ape!" Cynthia's mother screamed. "You only care about your job."

"No way, you venomous viper!" Cynthia's father answered. "You care only about your appearance. She's coming with me!"

Cynthia could barely stand the pain. She felt as if her arms might jolt out of her shoulder sockets if they pulled any harder.

Cynthia's mother used her mobile phone to contact her sister.

"Come over right away!" she pleaded. "It's an emergency. I need you!"

After a short while, Cynthia's Aunt Jude and her boyfriend, Wesley, arrived. They immediately began to pull on Cynthia's mother's side.

It seemed certain that they would win, with two extra people, but Cynthia's father used his mobile phone to call his friends Luke and Andy.

When they arrived, they joined in on Cynthia's

father's side, and the contest was evened out again.

"Let go, you beast!" Cynthia's mother whined.

"No, you let go, you evil-eyed crone!" Cynthia's father wailed.

Nobody even noticed that Cynthia was weeping and weeping, her agony almost unbearable.

Cynthia's mother looked around to see if she could get extra help from anywhere.

"Come and help us, Beatrix!" she called to her bulldog.

The bulldog waddled over and tugged at her belt. The extra weight was helpful.

"Here, Enid! Help my side!" Cynthia's father called to his rottweiler.

The dog waddled over and added his weight to Cynthia's father side.

Can you imagine what Cynthia was feeling? The pain overwhelmed her small body.

The noise of the people (and dogs) pulling and tugging and yanking and heaving and shouting and screaming and yelling and bellowing was finally heard by a policeman passing the house outside.

"Hello, hello!" he said. "What's going on in here then?"

"He wants to take my daughter away from me!" Cynthia's mother explained.

"She's lying!" Cynthia's father roared. "She wants to take my daughter from me!"

"Well, I tell you what," the policeman suggested. "The law has to be fair-minded about this. I'll draw a line in chalk here on the floor and when I say,

'Ready, steady, go!' both sides will pull. Whichever team pulls the other over this line is the winner and the daughter will stay with that person. Is that clear?"

Cynthia's mother and father both agreed. Nobody heard Cynthia's desperate protest – she was so frightened.

"Right now – ready, steady ... go!"

Both teams pulled and yanked and tugged and heaved.

First, Cynthia's mother's side appeared to be winning and almost pulled Cynthia's father's side over the chalked line. But then Cynthia's father's side was inspired by a fresh burst of energy and they almost pulled Cynthia's mother's side over the winning line.

Nobody noticed that Cynthia was in a terrible state.

The contest continued evenly for a while with both sides pulling and yanking and tugging and heaving, until suddenly, both sides pulled so hard that they split poor Cynthia clean down the middle!

There was a terrible shriek of pain, then each team fell noisily into a heap on different sides of the chalk line.

Cynthia's mother was still holding the left half of Cynthia, and Cynthia's father still held Cynthia's right half.

Cynthia's heart, however, fell out of her body and landed exactly on the chalk line.

The policeman picked it up and placed it in a

plastic bag. "The law will take this heart into its safekeeping, thank you very much," he announced. "And I now declare that the left half of the daughter belongs to the mother and the right half to the father. This proves, yet again, how fair-minded the law is."

Cynthia's father was happy with the outcome. He stormed out of the house holding Cynthia's right half.

"At last!" he said. "We can go find somewhere else to live!"

"I don't want to go anywhere without my other half!" Cynthia's right half shouted.

But her father ignored her and kept on going.

Cynthia's left half remained with her mother.

"We can be quite happy on our own," her mother said.

"But I want my other half back!" Cynthia's left half cried.

"Shush! Shush!" her mother said. "Let's give it a try."

Cynthia's father bought a flat in the centre of the city where he and Cynthia's right half could live. He bought her lots of presents and paid for her to have singing lessons. But it was so difficult to buy clothes for half a daughter or to have a sensible conversation with half a daughter.

Cynthia's mother tried to bake cakes with Cynthia's left half and she encouraged her to plant a vegetable garden. But Cynthia's mother also found it difficult to have good times with half a daughter or to find a suitable school for half a daughter to attend.

Each of Cynthia's halves was so unhappy. Neither could get used to being just half a person. Without a heart, neither Cynthia's left half, nor her right half, was able to enjoy anything anymore.

At her mother's house, Cynthia's left half had to hop, hop, hop to her school or to the shops or to the park and she found it difficult to make friends. Cynthia's left half was so unhappy that she cried many tears from her left eye.

At her father's flat, Cynthia's right half had to hop, hop, hop to a different school or to a different shop or a different park and she also found it difficult to make friends. Cynthia's right half was as unhappy as her left, and she cried just as many tears from her right eye.

Oh, how her left half and her right half longed for each other! The left half wrote long letters to the right half, explaining how much she missed her. And the right half replied, with long letters about the good times they used to have when Cynthia was one person.

Perhaps they could have lived separately until both Cynthia's halves were old ladies, wrinkled and using a walking stick to hop wherever they wanted to go. But one day Cynthia's mother was sitting downstairs in the kitchen when she noticed drip, drip, drip – the ceiling was leaking! She rushed upstairs to find it was Cynthia's left half weeping so much that there was a deep pool of tears on the floor!

"This has to stop!" she said, comforting Cynthia's left half. "I will contact your father immediately!" And she did.

But the phone at Cynthia's father's flat just rang and rang, for at that very moment

he was busy wiping up a pool of tears which Cynthia's right half had just wept. Eventually he answered.

"Listen to me," Cynthia's mother said. "This situation can't continue. We must glue Cynthia's two halves together again."

"Well, you bring your half here," Cynthia's father suggested. "Then we'll fit them together again."

"No way!" Cynthia's mother objected. "You bring your half here."

"Never, you obstinate hag!" Cynthia's father said.

"You're the same stubborn fool you always were!" Cynthia's mother replied.

There was an awful silence.

Then Cynthia's left half said to her mother, "What about my heart?"

And Cynthia's right half said to her father, "Why don't we all meet at the police station?"

So that's what they did.

"We've come for our daughter's heart," Cynthia's mother explained to the duty policeman.

"You'll both have to sign for it," the policeman said.

Cynthia's parents signed the heart register. The policeman went downstairs to the vault which he unlocked with a large key. There in the vault was a glass case and in the glass case was Cynthia's heart – still beating!

"Here it is!" the policeman said, handing it over. "Still in good shape!"

"I'll take it," Cynthia's father said.

"No way, you sly fox!" Cynthia's mother shouted. "Here, give it to me!"

"Never, you treacherous jackal!" Cynthia's father yelled.

"Excuse me," the policeman butted in. "I will handle this matter fairly and squarely."

He made Cynthia's mother stand on one side with Cynthia's left half, and Cynthia's father stand on the other with Cynthia's right half.

"Now, wait for my command!"

He searched in his first-aid kit for a tube of special glue which policemen always keep handy for these occasions.

"Okay," he said to Cynthia's mother and father. "Now carefully bring your daughter's two halves together."

As they did so, the policeman slotted in Cynthia's heart. It fitted snugly. Then he glued her two halves together.

Cynthia's parents were pleased to have their daughter whole again. They thanked the policeman for his help.

"It's all part of our line of duties. I'm glad to have been of service."

Cynthia and her parents turned to leave.

"From now on," Cynthia's mother said to her father, "she will live with me and you can have her every second weekend."

"No way, you poxy slug!" Cynthia's father protested, grabbing her by the right arm. "She's coming to live with me and you can have her every second weekend."

"You verminous rat!" Cynthia's mother snarled, taking hold of her daughter's left arm.

As they began to pull, Cynthia's two halves began to come unstuck again.

"Ouch!" Cynthia cried. She called for the policeman, who came running with the tube of special glue. He ordered Cynthia's parents to stop tugging. When they had loosened their grip, he glued her two halves where they were coming unstuck.

"Can I keep that glue?" Cynthia asked. "It may come in handy."

"Certainly," the policeman answered, giving her the tube.

Cynthia walked out of the police station with her mother and father. Immediately, her mother wanted to turn left, whereas her father wanted to turn right.

"She's coming home with me first!" her mother screamed.

"She's not!" her father bellowed. "She's coming with me, you impossible shrew!"

"Listen!" Cynthia said. "If you both don't stop

screaming, I'll seal your mouths shut with this special glue. From now on, you are going to stop calling each other names or I'll never live with either of you."

Cynthia's mother and father were startled. They looked at each other and wondered how on earth they could change their ways.

"Alright," her mother said. "Let's spin a coin to see who she goes with first. Heads it's you, tails me."

"That's fine!" her father agreed. "I'll spin the coin."

From then on, Cynthia spent some time each week with her mother and some time each week with her father. She was able to be a whole person no matter who she was with. Never again was she torn in two. Nor did her parents dare hurl abuse at each other – at least, not when Cynthia was around!

In the years that followed, her wounds began to heal. But even to this day, she still has a scar all the way down her middle, where she once was split in half. However, her heart has grown stronger with every hour that's passed and the last I heard from her, she felt she had a good chance of living happily ever after.

Craig and his brother, Mouse, lived with their mum who had a night job. Every evening when she went off to work, she hugged them and always said the same thing:

"Don't open the door and don't go out,
There's plenty of danger and trouble about."

Then she would give them each a kiss and say:

"Look after yourselves, no need to roam,
Stay happy and snug until I come home."

These words always kept the brothers warm and cosy until their mum returned some time after midnight. Craig was the older of the two brothers, so he was supposed to look after Mouse. And mostly he did. They would eat their dinner and watch some TV, then Mouse would go up to bed. Craig would stay down a while, mucking about with this and that, before he too would go to sleep. Later, they would hear the familiar sound of the key in the front door. Their mum would come upstairs, peep in to each of their rooms, and say:

"I'm home at last, are my boys all right?
I love you both, sleep well, good night."

But one dark and drearisome night, their mum was in a rush to go to work.

"Oh dear, oh dear!" she said. "I must hurry! Where's my coat?"

She found the coat with the furry collar, pulled it on, and ran out of the house without hugging or kissing her boys. Nor did she speak the words which would keep them warm and cosy until she returned.

Next thing, the doorbell rang. It was Doog, the older lad from up the hill who carried a knife in his pocket. One day he had shown Craig and Mouse how he could spin it up in the air and catch it again by the handle.

"Coming out?" Doog asked. "We'll have fun."

"No!" Craig replied. "I have to look after my brother."

"Bring him along too!" Doog said.

"I don't want to go out," Mouse said.

"Come on, it'll be fun!" Craig urged.

So Craig and Mouse put on their warm jackets and out they went into the dark and drearisome night.

First stop was the Newt and Spider, a place where

they met up with Lloyd, who pretended to be old enough to buy drinks. Craig and Mouse waited outside.

A while later, Doog emerged carrying a couple of beers.

"Here!" he said, passing one to Craig.

Craig lifted the mug to his lips and swallowed some of the bitter tasting drink.

"Give some to the kid!" Doog said.

"No way," Craig replied. "He's too young."

So Craig drank the rest of the beer and he felt oozy-woozy by the end of it.

Doog and Lloyd drank without seeming to feel anything. When they had finished the first drink, they bought another. And another. The more they drank the noisier they became, swearing and bragging and boasting.

"Let's go do a house!" Lloyd suggested.

Doog agreed, so they all walked up the road to the estate. Craig's walking was a bit wobbly and he could barely keep a straight line. He felt sick. Lloyd and Doog weren't that much better. From time to time, they staggered against walls or tripped on the pavement.

"Here's number 73," Lloyd said. "The owners are away."

"You two keep watch," Doog told Craig and Mouse. "If anyone comes, whistle!"

Lloyd and Doog went around the back of the house. Craig and Mouse heard glass breaking.

"Let's go home!" Mouse whimpered. "I'm cold!"

"We can't go now," Craig said. "When they're finished with the house we'll go."

"Yes," Mouse said. "I'm tired."

After what seemed like a long time, Lloyd and Doog came out of the front door of the house. Lloyd was carrying a video-camera he had found inside. Doog was carrying keys. He used them to open the garage at the side of the house. Then he opened the door of the car, started the engine and reversed out.

"Climb in!" he said.

"We have to go now," Craig said. "My brother's cold and tired."

"No problem," Doog said. "I'll drop you off at your house."

"But you're drunk!" Craig pointed out. "You shouldn't drive!"

Doog laughed.

"Who says? I'm fine. Climb in!"

"I don't want to," Mouse whispered to Craig.

"It's okay, it's just a short ride to our house," Craig replied.

So Craig and Mouse climbed into the back of the car. Lloyd sat in the front next to Doog.

Doog revved the engine until it roared ferociously. Then he drove off at high speed. But he didn't go anywhere near the area where Craig and Mouse lived. Instead, he drove them though the city, screeching around the curves. It was wild and Mouse was frightened.

"I told you I'm a good driver!" Doog boasted. "Isn't this excellent? I should enter the Grand

Prix." He drove the car past the docks area, then up through the trading estate.

Craig noticed a car behind them. He realised they were being followed.

"Police!" he shouted. "Stop, Doog, or we'll be in dead trouble!"

"Na! We'll lose them!" Doog replied.

He swung the car suddenly to the right, went the wrong way around the roundabout, and turned off down a street of shops. He thought he'd dodged the police, but when he looked round, there was the blue light, still following them.

By the time Doog looked back at the road, the car had mounted the pavement with a huge jolt. He tried to swing the car round to avoid crashing into the shops, but somehow it swung round too much and rolled over. It rolled and rolled, then crashed into a brick wall.

Glass shattered, a few bricks came tumbling down, smoke rose from the car in the yellow street-lights. Then there was silence.

Craig hurt. A blue light was flashing on and off. Craig drifted up out of the car. He was floating. He floated above the car. He could see it there in the yellow light. He could see Doog and Lloyd running off. And there was Mouse lying motionless on the back seat. And still Craig floated. If he moved his left hand, he floated to the left. And if he moved his right hand, he floated to the right. If he lifted his head he flew upwards, and if he looked down, he flew downwards. And now he was so high, he could see the city below him, with its yellow streetlights and tall office blocks and, stretching away in the distance, rows of houses, and then the countryside in darkness.

But what was that flying towards him? As it approached, Craig could see it was a man in a black cloak, heading in the direction of the crashed car.

"Hey, where are you going?" Craig asked the man.

"To collect the kid," the cloaked figure answered.

'"But you can't!" Craig cried.

"Give me three good reasons why I can't!" the figure said.

Craig was confused. He couldn't think of anything.

"Well, see you later!" the figure said, and flew down towards the car.

Craig hovered where he was for a while. Then he moved his left hand and flew over the docks, across the estate, towards the house they had lived in before, where he and Mouse had lived with their Mum and Geoff, their dad. That was before Geoff walked out on them.

He floated down, down, down to the house and drifted in through the back window, his old bedroom window, where he could see a young boy sitting on the bed. It was himself when he was younger.

Geoff came in and said to the young Craig, "Hi there! How are you doing?"

The young boy hugged his father and said, "Dad,

please don't walk out on us. I'll always love you."

"Who said I'm gonna walk out? I'll never do that," his dad said.

"Oh yes, you will," the boy said. "You're gonna go to Canada and leave us here."

Geoff said goodnight to the young Craig and went out of the room.

Craig floated out of the bedroom to the landing and watched his father go into the big bedroom where his mum was. Then he heard them arguing. "Don't touch me!" his mum screamed. Eventually Geoff said, "I'm off to Canada. I've had enough of all this."

As his dad came out of the big bedroom, Craig floated towards him and said angrily, "See! I knew you were going to leave!" Geoff put his arm around the boy and said, "Good luck, son!" Then he took a small model of a starship from his pocket and gave it to Craig. "Take care of Mouse for me, won't you? I love you both."

Craig heard his mum sobbing and weeping and the front door shut as Geoff walked out for ever and ever, never to come back.

Craig put the model starship in his own pocket, then floated up out of his bedroom window. He could see his dad driving off, heading for the airport. Craig floated over the city, using his left hand to turn left, and his right hand to turn right, lifting his head to fly upwards and lowering his head to fly downwards. He flew across the city until he saw below him a lady walking along the pavement in the dark and drearisome night, wearing a coat with a furry collar. She reached a house, put a key in the door and stepped inside.

"That's our mum!" Craig thought, "and that's the house where we live now." He lowered his head and flew down, down, down to the house and then he flew in through his bedroom window.

His mother came up the stairs, peeped in his bedroom door as she always did, and Craig heard her say:

"I'm home at last, are my boys all right?
I love you both, sleep well, good night."

But when she looked in Mouse's bedroom, she gasped in shock.

"Mouse? Where are you?" she cried.

She came running back into Craig's bedroom.

"Where's Mouse?" she asked. "Is he alright?"

"I know where he is," Craig sniffed, tears rolling down his cheeks.

"My darling child!" his mum wailed. "Why didn't you look after him?"

"I'll go get him back!" Craig mumbled.

"Here," his mum said, "you may need this."

She gave him a mouth-organ, the one Mouse liked to play. He was good with music, Mouse was.

Craig put the mouth-organ in his pocket, next to the starship his dad had given him. Then he raised his head and floated up, out of the window, into the night sky.

"Bring Mouse back safely to me!" he could hear his mum crying.

Craig floated over the city, using his left hand to turn left, and his right hand to turn right, lifting his head to fly upwards and lowering his head to fly downwards. And he flew across the estate, high above the yellow streetlights, until he saw someone running. It was a boy, running along, looking behind him as if the devil were chasing him.

Craig lowered his head, and down, down, down he flew until he was hovering over the boy. It was Doog. When he saw Craig floating in the air above him, he tripped and went sprawling onto the pavement.

"It's all your fault!" Craig shouted.

"It wasn't!" Doog replied. "I'm a good driver! It was the car's fault! Something was wrong with the steering!"

Craig floated closer towards Doog.

"Don't you dare touch me!" Doog said, pulling the knife out of his pocket.

Craig wasn't frightened. He suddenly flew towards Doog and kicked the knife out of his hand. Then he floated down and picked up the knife himself. He put it in his pocket, next to the starship his dad given him and the mouth-organ given to him by his mother.

Craig floated up into the night sky. He saw two policemen running after Doog and catching him. Then he floated across the docks area, using his left hand to turn left, and his right hand to turn right, lifting his head to fly upwards and lowering his head to fly downwards. Eventually he saw the crashed car way below him. Would he be in time? He lowered his head, and floated down, down, down, through the open back door, into the crashed car.

Oh no! The man with the black cloak was lifting Mouse from the seat.

"Leave him alone!" Craig said.

"It's too late!" the man replied. "I already have him in my arms."

Craig was desperate. He tried to pull Mouse out of the man's clutch, but it was impossible.

"Please don't take my brother away!" Craig shouted.

"Give me three good reasons why I shouldn't!" the man said.

"Because his dad loves him, his mum loves him and I love him!" Craig screamed.

The man in the cloak hesitated.

"Why should I believe you?" he asked.

"Please!" Craig pleaded. "These three things will prove it." And he fetched the starship, the mouthorgan and Doog's knife from his pocket and showed them to the man.

"Alright, kid!" the man said. "But next time, I won't be so soft."

The cloaked man replaced Mouse on the seat of the car. Then he climbed out of the car and flew off into the night sky.

Craig was relieved. He rested his head on Mouse's shoulder.

A while later he became slowly aware of sirens whining. Blue and red lights were flashing.

"This one's coming round now," a voice was saying.

He was being lifted onto a stretcher.

"Where's Mouse?" Craig asked. "Is he alright?"

"I'm here," Mouse said. He was in the ambulance, bandaged. "Can we go home now?"

"Okay, you two?" one of the ambulance men said, climbing in and shutting the doors. "We're off to the hospital now to have you checked over. We phoned your mum. She'll meet us there."

Secrets of Lizard Magic

In a city to the west of everywhere lived a man with two sons, Luke and Vincent, and a young daughter, Fran, who was her father's delight.

The man had been stricken with a terrible illness. Doctors examined him and prescribed various treatments, but without success. They declared there was nothing more they could do to save him and that he had just a few months to live.

"Surely there must be a cure for this," Fran said to her brothers. "A remedy somewhere that would help."

"I doubt it," Luke said. "The doctors have tried everything."

"If the doctors can't save him, nothing will," Vincent added.

When their father became so ill that he could barely sit up in bed, Fran finally persuaded Luke to go search for a remedy.

To tell the truth, Luke didn't want to leave the city. He enjoyed hanging out in bars and nightclubs. He wasn't keen to venture out into the wilds on a foolish errand, but he reckoned that he'd be back soon enough. His father gave him a wallet of cash and advised him to spend it wisely.

Luke boarded a train heading east. He travelled overnight to a small town at the edge of the wilderness. His backpack filled with supplies, he set off towards an area renowned for its medicine men. After several days he found himself in an arid desert, where the only plants which grew were round cactuses, flat cactuses, hairy cactuses and prickly cactuses. Day after day he trudged along without seeing another person. Before long, he had consumed all the food from his backpack and was forced to snare small desert creatures and drink cactus juice. But he never managed to fill his belly and what he longed for more than anything was a satisfying meal. Finally, he reached a lumpy outcrop of mountains known as the Devil's Backbone.

"At last!" he said. "A bit of shade and possibly a jackrabbit for my lunch."

About half way up the mountain he stumbled over a smooth rock. Or at least he thought it was a rock, until, on closer inspection, it turned out to be an egg.

How extraordinary it was! Larger than an ostrich egg and with a shell as transparent as plastic film.

Inside the egg was a pinkish jelly in which a strange creature lay curled. Its eyes were closed, but clearly its heart was beating and blood circulated through its arteries.

"What a piece of luck," Luke thought. "Here I am, not having eaten a decent meal for weeks and what should I find, but just the sort of egg that would make a wonderful omelette. But how can I eat it without a decent frying pan?"

From his rucksack he fetched out a telescope which he raised to one eye. He surveyed the surrounding countryside. A long way off, he spied a small building.

Hastily he made his way down the Devil's Backbone into the valley. Above the front door of the building was a sign: LAST CHANCE SUPPLY STORE. He stepped inside.

"What can I do for you, fellow?" the storekeeper inquired.

"Do you sell frying pans?" Luke asked.

"Sure do," the storekeeper replied.

He waded through the shelves of sleeping bags, thermal underwear and pocket knives to the wall on the opposite end of the shop where dinghies were hanging alongside flashlights and kettles. He pushed these aside and there, sure enough, was a frying pan. But how small it was, Luke thought.

"Don't you have something larger?" he asked.

The storekeeper searched again and on another wall he found a frying pan twice the size of the first.

"That's better," Luke said, "but a larger one would be better still."

"Well, we may have something bigger round the back," the storekeeper said.

Luke heard the man clattering around in the storeroom. Finally he emerged, with the largest frying pan that Luke had ever seen.

"This big enough?" the man asked.

"Yes, that will do nicely," Luke nodded. "How much does it cost?"

The storekeeper mentioned a very large amount of money.

"But that's all I've got," Luke said.

"Listen, mister, you won't get another frying pan like this until you've crossed the desert. Solid iron, this is."

"Okay, I'll take it."

Luke gave the storekeeper all his money and tied the frying pan to his back.

The walk back to the egg was extremely strenuous, not only because it was uphill, but because of the enormous weight of the frying pan. He was within sight of where he had left the egg when he heard the sound of hooves. Twelve men were approaching on twelve black horses. They were masked bandits!

"What have we here?" they asked each other.

"Looks like enough for an evening meal."

Luke quaked in his boots.

"You can't eat me!" he wailed.

"Why not?" the bandits replied. "Food isn't easy to come by in these here parts."

"Please," Luke pleaded. "I'm not tasty."

"The proof of the pudding is in the eating," one of the bandits said, and the others chuckled.

"What's that on your back?" they asked.

"A frying pan," Luke answered. "If you let me go you can have it."

The bandits laughed. "The evening meal comes complete with its own frying pan! Fried meat tonight, lads!"

"Please..." Luke begged.

"Well, we could let you go if you hand over your loot!"

"I don't have any left!" he wailed.

"Tough luck, sonny boy!" they said. And they carried him, pan and all, to their den on the northern slope of the Devil's Backbone.

Back home, Luke's father was becoming anxious. With every day that passed he grew feebler.

"Luke's been away ages and still no word from him," he said.

Vincent, like his older brother, didn't want to leave the city. He enjoyed accompanying his older brother to bars and nightclubs. But now, without his brother, it wasn't so much fun. So off he went. His father gave him a wallet containing the same amount of money he had given Luke and the same words of advice to spend it wisely.

Vincent boarded the train which took him to the small wilderness town. Then he followed Luke's trail until he found himself in the same arid desert where the only plants which grew were round cactuses, flat cactuses, hairy cactuses and prickly cactuses. Finally he reached the Devil's Backbone where he, too, stumbled over the large egg. He noticed the creature curled inside it, with its closed eyes and beating heart.

"What a piece of luck," Vincent thought. "Here I am, starvingly hungry, and what should I find, but just the sort of egg that would taste wonderful hard-boiled. But how can I cook it without a decent pot?"

From his rucksack he fetched out a telescope which he raised to one eye. In the valley he spied the Last Chance Supply Store. Down the mountain-side he ran, imagining how delicious the large egg would taste.

"Do you sell pots?" Vincent inquired.

"Sure do," the storekeeper said.

After much searching he produced a small pot.

"Don't you have something larger?" Vincent enquired.

The storekeeper found a pot twice the size of the first.

"That's better," Vincent said, "but a larger one would be better still."

The storekeeper fetched from the storeroom the largest pot that Vincent had ever seen.

"This big enough?" the man asked.

"Yes, that will do," Vincent nodded.

When he heard how much it cost, he hesitated.

"Listen, mister, you won't get another iron pot like this around here."

"Okay, I'll take it."

Vincent gave the storekeeper all his money and tied the pot to his back.

He staggered up the mountainside weighed down by the enormous pot. He had almost reached the egg when he heard the sound of hooves. Twelve masked bandits were approaching on twelve black horses!

"Look lads!" the bandits shouted. "The evening stew comes complete with its own pot!!"

"Please don't eat me!" Vincent begged.

"Do you have any loot to buy your freedom?"

"No," Vincent wailed. "I spent it all on the pot."

"Tough luck!" the bandits laughed. And they carried him, pot and all, to their den.

With no news of either Luke or Vincent, their father grew increasingly anxious about the fate of his sons. He was now so ill, he had difficulty breathing.

"Should I try to find them?" Fran asked him.

"No way," her father said. "A girl out on the roads! It's too dangerous."

But Fran insisted. She wasn't keen to leave her father. But she was anxious to go off and find a remedy which would restore him to good health.

In the end, he relented. Ill as he was, he gave her a wallet containing the same amount of money as each of her brothers had received and advised her to spend it wisely.

Fran took the train east, then crossed the wilderness, following the trail of her brothers. After several days she came to the arid desert, where the only plants which grew were round cactuses, flat cactuses, hairy cactuses and prickly cactuses. Finally she reached the Devil's Backbone where she, too, stumbled over the large egg.

"How extraordinary!" Fran thought, as she examined it closely. She was fascinated by the small curled-up creature she could see in the centre of the egg, with its closed eyes and beating heart.

"What a piece of luck," she thought. "I must wait here until it hatches, for surely something marvellous will come of this."

She pulled her sleeping bag from her rucksack and wrapped it around the egg. Then she lay down, huddled against the egg, and waited patiently.

How long she slept, she never knew. But she was woken by the sound of clattering hooves. There before her were the twelve masked bandits on their twelve black horses!

"A girl this time!" they exclaimed. "Our luck's in, guys!"

"We've eaten two men," they explained to Fran. "And now it's your turn, unless you have money to buy your freedom."

"I do," Fran said.

"How much?" the bandits enquired.

"Enough," Fran said, and she handed over her wallet.

The bandits greedily divided the notes amongst themselves.

"Not bad," they said. "We'll spare your life. But

you still have to come with us to our den to be our maid."

"Never!" Fran cried.

They were just about to take her by force, when one of them noticed the large lump in her sleeping bag.

"What's that? Take it out!" they ordered.

"No!" she said.

"Open it up or you're done for!" the bandits yelled, pulling out their six-shooters and aiming at her.

Carefully, Fran lifted the egg out of the sleeping bag. The bandits could barely hide their excitement.

"What an egg!" they shouted. "Let's take it back to our den and fry half in the pan and boil the other half in the pot."

"You will do nothing of the sort!" Fran said. "Because it's just about to hatch."

Sure enough, there, right in front of their eyes, the transparent shell began to crack!

A claw poked through. Bits of shell broke away. Jelly seeped from the egg onto the ground. A second claw poked through, followed by a tail! Then the egg snapped in two and the rest of the creature rolled out onto the ground.

It was scaly, pink and black. The creature began to uncurl itself, rising onto its legs, then standing upright. Slowly, it unfolded its body until it was as tall as a man! Finally, the lizard creature lifted up its head. And what a head it was! With huge round eyes, gleaming, darting to the left and right, and a forked tongue which shot out every now and then.

Fran and the bandits could barely believe their eyes!

But if they were surprised by its appearance, they were flabbergasted when it now began to speak to Fran.

"I am Ixpetz, the Bright-Eyed. You have saved my life, now I will help you. Let us walk."

The twelve masked bandits thought about blocking his way, but Ixpetz shot out his forked tongue and emitted an ear-curdling hiss.

The bandits replaced their guns in their holsters.

Ixpetz, the Bright-Eyed, spoke again to Fran.

"Keep me always within your sight,
Let your footsteps follow my track.
Turn neither to the left nor right
And never look back."

Then Ixpetz walked boldly past the masked bandits. Fran followed close behind, keeping her eyes fixed on him. The bandits were rooted to the spot and didn't try to stop them.

Once they were safe, Fran told Ixpetz about her father who was languishing with a terrible illness.

"The doctors can't help him," she explained. "I must find a remedy, otherwise he'll die within a few months."

She then told Ixpetz about her brothers, how they had failed to return home and were now missing.

"Come!" Ixpetz said. "First we will find your brothers. Then we will see about healing your father."

Fran was filled with hope. She knew there was a remedy somewhere that could cure her father, and if anyone could help her, it was this extraordinary lizard.

After some time they came to a disused mine cut into the mountainside. Ixpetz entered the darkness. Fran followed. The smell was awful, a mixture of horse manure and unwashed socks and underwear. There were twelve filthy sleeping bags in a row and Fran realised that this must be the bandits' den.

Beyond the sleeping quarters stood a huge pot and a huge pan. Next to each of these was a pile of bones. Ixpetz, the Bright-Eyed, stepped up to each pile and blew on it. Instantly Fran saw her two older brothers Luke and Vincent, standing as whole as ever they stood. She was amazed to see them alive again.

"Whew!" they said. "That was a close call. We were nearly eaten by bandits."

When the brothers laid eyes on the giant lizard they nearly fainted.

"Who's this?" they whispered to Fran.

"This is Ixpetz, who has saved our lives," Fran explained. "Now he's going to help us find a cure for our father."

"Let us walk!" Ixpetz said.

"We'll just take some of the bandits' loot before we go," the two brothers said.

They seized handfuls of money from the tin box in which the bandits stored their stolen wealth. Ixpetz shot out his forked tongue and emitted an ear-curdling hiss. The two older brothers hurriedly pocketed what they had grabbed and left the mine.

They walked for what seemed like weeks. The brothers, weighed down by the coins, grumbled about the difficulties of the journey. Eventually they emerged from a canyon onto the open plains, where they found themselves in the middle of a tumultuous hubbub and commotion. Two armies were spread out as far as the eye could see, one in red uniforms to the left and the other in green uniforms to the right. Tanks, missile launchers, cannon and guns were firing from left to right and right to left.

Ixpetz, the Bright-Eyed, strode directly straight between the two armies.

"Where are you going?" Luke yelled.

"You can't just walk down the middle of a battle-field!" Vincent shouted.

But Ixpetz shot out his forked tongue and emitted an ear-curdling hiss.

"Keep me always within your sight,
Let your footsteps follow my track.
Turn neither to the left nor right
And never look back."

So Fran, Luke and Vincent followed as closely as they could.

When they were about halfway across, it occurred to Luke that the red army's cause was just. He veered off to the left and joined in the battle. At precisely the same time it occurred to Vincent that the green army's cause was just. He veered off to the right and also took up arms.

"Your brothers are hasty to meet their fate," Ixpetz said.

Luke and Vincent fought for the opposing armies all day and by evening both had been severely injured.

In the meantime Ixpetz walked on and Fran followed.

The next day a Red Cross ambulance overtook them. Ixpetz hailed the driver and asked to see the wounded. Luke and Vincent were in there, but showing no sign of life.

Ixpetz, the Bright-Eyed, blew first in Luke's ear, then in Vincent's ear and both brothers leaped out of the ambulance.

"Whew! That was a close shave," they said. "We were nearly killed in battle."

Fran was grateful to see her brothers restored to life.

Ixpetz led Fran and her brothers beyond the commotion of battle. Soon they were alone again in the midst of arid desert, where the only plants which grew were round cactuses, flat cactuses, hairy cactuses and prickly cactuses. For an age they wandered here and there, the brothers becoming more and more irritable in the merciless heat of the sun.

"I'm thirsty," Luke said. "I'm tired of cactus juice."

"And I'm scorched by this accursed sun," Vincent said. "Will we never reach shade?"

"We must keep going!" Fran insisted. "He promised to find a remedy for our father."

The brothers moaned to each other as the days passed. And as they became hungrier and thirstier, their moods worsened.

"He doesn't know where he's taking us," Luke said.

"He's as lost as we are," Vincent added.

Perhaps Ixpetz, the Bright-Eyed, heard their grumblings, but all he said was:

"Keep me always within your sight,
Let your footsteps follow my track.
Turn neither to the left nor to the right
And never look back."

Not long after this, an astonishing sight greeted Luke's eyes – an oasis up ahead on the left, with elegant palm trees surrounding a clear pool of water. A beautiful woman wearing a swimming costume and dark glasses lounged on a sunbed. In her belly button was a glittering topaz.

"Brother, my luck has changed!" Luke said.

"Mine too!" said Vincent, for at that moment he too spied an oasis, up ahead on the right, where another girl lounged on a sunbed. In her belly button a sapphire gleamed.

They ran off, Luke to the left and Vincent to the right.

Ixpetz shot out his forked tongue and emitted an ear-curdling hiss.

"We will return for you in three days," he shouted.

Fran followed Ixpetz across the sands.

"Your brothers stubbornly refuse to learn," he said. "But you have done well. I will now teach you the five secrets of lizard magic."

During the next three days, on a high dune, Ixpetz, the Bright-Eyed, showed Fran how to walk on the earth without leaving a trail, how to see without looking, how to avoid danger by remaining motionless, how to be awake while sleeping and how to seek advice from the lizard-spirits.

Fran learned eagerly and Ixpetz was pleased.

"Let us go rescue your brothers one last time," he said. "And tomorrow I will give you the remedy for your father's illness."

Ixpetz led Fran through the deserts until two garish buildings came in sight. The building on the left was called Luke's Casino and the one on the right Vincent's Casino. In the lush gardens of each was a turquoise swimming pool surrounded by elegant palm trees.

But what a wailing could be heard coming from within each casino!

Ixpetz and Fran entered Luke's Casino first. Inside, the woman with a topaz in her belly button was wailing beside a coffin.

"He's dead!" she cried.

Fran looked in the coffin and saw Luke.

"What happened?" she asked the woman.

"He was shot by gamblers," she replied.

Ixpetz, the Bright-Eyed, leaned into the coffin, blew in the man's ear and immediately Luke jumped out of his coffin, alive and well!

"Whew!" he said. "That was a close call."

Then they all went across to Vincent's Casino, where a similar scene was taking place.

"Vince is dead!" the woman with the sapphire in her belly button wailed.

"What happened?" Fran asked.

"He was shot by moneylenders."

Ixpetz blew in the dead man's ear and immediately Vincent jumped out of his coffin.

"Whew!" he said. "What a narrow escape!"

Fran was glad to see her brothers alive again.

"Let us walk!" Ixpetz, the Bright-Eyed, said. "We are nearly at our journey's end."

He headed out across the sands. Fran followed.

"We can't leave here," Luke whispered.

"We'll return after we've delivered the remedy to our father," Vincent agreed.

Ixpetz shot out his forked tongue and emitted an ear-curdling hiss.

"Keep me always within your sight,
Let your footsteps follow my track.
Turn neither to the left nor to the right
And never look back."

The brothers followed Ixpetz. But how difficult it was!

"Oh no!" Luke said. "I can't face the desert again!"

"At least back there we had a life of luxury," Vincent added.

The two brothers still followed Ixpetz, but their pace slowed considerably.

"This isn't a good idea," Luke said. "We could make a fortune in those casinos."

"I agree," Vincent said. "Every minute wasted is money lost."

Their walking came to a stop. They could no longer contain themselves. They turned around and looked back!

But what did they see?

No oases! No casinos! No palm trees! No swimming pools! Nothing!

Only a barren desert, with round cactuses, flat cactuses, hairy cactuses and prickly cactuses.

"What happened?" Luke asked.

"Where's it all gone?" Vincent howled.

They ran back across the barren desert, searching the endless sands.

"Where's my casino?" Luke called out. "I'm sure it was just about here."

"I think mine was in front of that sand dune," Vincent replied. "Or was it on the far side?"

Fran could hear their voices getting softer as they disappeared into the distance, searching this way and that for their lost casinos. But she never once looked back.

Ixpetz walked onwards and Fran followed. The next evening, they reached a sunken valley, scattered with stone ruins.

Ixpetz crossed the stone maze until he reached a garden, where the strangest cactuses were growing.

He cut leaves and branches from several of these before proceeding to the stone circle at the centre of the maze. He asked Fran to light a great fire.

"This is a place of dancing," Ixpetz, the Bright-Eyed, said. He laid the leaves and branches on a flat stone which was being heated by the flames. Then he began to move around the circle, stomping his feet.

If you haven't ever seen a giant lizard dance, I can tell you it's an amazing sight! Ixpetz waved his tail behind him. He lifted his head to the dark sky and sang, "Ahuya! Huya! Huya!" He spun round and sang, "Aheeya! Heeya! Heeya!"

Fran felt her own legs aching to dance! She wanted to join in! So she did. She danced, twirled and stomped, and joyfully she sang, "Ahuya! Huya! Huya!" She spun round and jumped and sang, "Aheeya! Heeya! Heeya!"

The dancing continued for much of the evening, but suddenly Ixpetz stopped. It took Fran by surprise. He placed the dried-out cactus fragments in a stone bowl and ground them into a powder with a stone pestle.

"Here is the remedy for your father," Ixpetz said.

"Thank you! Thank you!" Fran said, with tears of gratitude welling in her eyes.

"I have brought you to this place," Ixpetz said. "The rest is up to you. The time has come for me to journey on alone"

The words pained Fran. She was stunned. She

had grown fond of Ixpetz and did not wish to be parted from him. But Ixpetz shot out his forked tongue and emitted an ear-curdling hiss.

"No!" he said. "You will make your own tracks from now on!"

And with that, Ixpetz stepped into the heart of the fire. The flames flared up all around him as high as the stars and moon – orange and green and mauve! The whole desert was lit up from end to end by the blaze.

Fran stood and stared. Sparks cascaded out in all directions. It was awesome! She gazed at the searing flames which leaped into the night sky and, as she did so, their brightness entered her own eyes. The longer she stared, the brighter her eyes shone, until they gleamed as brilliantly as the fire itself. Even when the flames eventually died down, Fran's eyes were still glowing.

It was only then that she realised how weary she was. She lay down on the stone ruins and slept. She was alone. There was not a single trace left of Ixpetz, the Bright-Eyed.

The following morning, Fran gathered the healing powder into a leather pouch and left the ruins, walking in a westerly direction, determined to return to her father with the remedy before it was too late. She had no one to watch out for her now. But knowing the five secrets of lizard magic, she felt confident.

The desert was scorching hot during the day and

freezing cold at night. She knew there were bandits out there, snakes and spiders with deadly bites, as well as ravenous coyotes and vultures. One desert hill looked much like another – it was easy to get lost or travel in circles without knowing it. But Fran walked without leaving a trail, she saw without looking, she avoided danger by remaining motionless, she kept awake at night while sleeping and she sought advice from the lizard-spirits.

In this way, she survived. Several days later she reached the town at the edge of the wilderness. She boarded the overnight train and finally arrived back in the city to the west of everywhere.

People stopped to gaze at her – they had never seen anyone with such large, glowing eyes! They moved aside as she approached. Fran, the Bright-Eyed, had returned!

She made her way hastily through the familiar streets towards the hospital, where she found her father at the point of death. His face was ashen, his eyes were closed. She took a quantity of powder from the pouch. She smeared it on her father's forehead and on the palms of his hands.

After a while he opened his eyes.

"You have returned, dear child," he said.

He embraced his daughter rapturously.

Within hours he was sitting up in bed. Later, his appetite for food returned. The following morning he was able to stand on his own. He tried taking a few steps, leaning on Fran's arm, and soon was walking around unaided.

The doctors were astonished by his recovery. It was not long before they agreed that he was well enough to be released from hospital.

Street Boy

The city where Hedley lived, like most other cities, sprawled out in all directions, with a huge number of inhabitants and streets which were always busy. For Hedley, it was home. He lived there with his father, mother and younger sister, Serena.

Their comfortable house overlooked a subway station and from his upstairs window Hedley could see the rush of commuters setting out every Monday to Friday for work. Each evening he would see them all return. It was like the tide of an ocean going out and in every day, waves of people flowing first in one direction, then the other.

Hedley was used to all this bustle happening on the other side of the road. He walked past the station in the morning on his way to school and he walked past it again on his way back home in the afternoon.

One day he noticed a boy no older than himself sitting on the pavement outside the station, with a scruffy dog beside him and a cap laid upside down in front of him with a few coins sprinkled in it. The boy looked like he didn't wash all that often and his clothes were shabby.

The boy was there again the following day and every day after that. Sometimes he'd be sitting there with his dog next to him, or he'd be talking to the newspaperman, an old fellow with no teeth who sat at a little table most of the time, selling the daily papers.

Hedley never spoke to the street boy, but every day on his way to and from school he saw him. Hedley also watched him from his upstairs window.

Very few people threw coins into the boy's cap, but some did, and every now and again the boy would remove several coins and slip them in his pocket. At night the street boy slept in the doorway of a shop which was boarded up and empty. He lay on a few sheets of cardboard and climbed into a dark green sleeping bag which had seen better years.

Hedley's parents had also noticed the street boy.

"This area's going downhill," Hedley's father complained.

"They shouldn't be allowed to beg there!" his mother groused.

But the boy was always there and near him, his faithful dog. The dog never wandered off on its own. It was a sort of white terrier with black markings. Actually not that white. More like yellowish brown. Once, Hedley saw them share a packet of crisps.

When Hedley's parents asked him what he wanted for his birthday, which was no more than a few weeks away, Hedley answered, "A dog."

"A dog's out of the question," his mother said. "There'd be nobody to look after it when we're at work and you're at school."

"Why don't you choose a bike," his father suggested. "Then you could ride to school."

So Hedley said, "Okay, a bike."

"I want a bike also," his little sister Serena pouted.

But before his birthday came along, the weather turned freezing cold. There was a shimmer of frost on the grass in the morning and puddles turned into sheets of ice which cracked if you stepped on them. Flurries of snow fell from time to time. Hedley wore his fur-lined anorak and put on gloves and a scarf to go to school.

The street boy huddled in his sleeping bag during the day, hugging his dog closely for extra warmth. Hedley thought it was unfair that the boy should be out there in the freezing cold.

"Can't we help him?" he asked his parents.

"I don't think so," his father answered. "It's his choice to live out there on the streets."

"Can't we at least give him some warmer clothes?" Hedley persisted.

"No!" his mother said adamantly. "Then he'd never stop pestering us for more."

The severe cold continued for sixteen days. A biting northern wind added to the misery of being outdoors.

From his upstairs window, Hedley looked down at the street boy and his dog. The boy was lying in a ball in his sleeping bag, with the dog curled up next to him.

Then, one morning, on his way to school, Hedley noticed that the boy wasn't there! The green sleeping bag was lying in a heap in the entrance of the boarded-up shop and the dog was lying on it, whining.

A feeling of panic rushed through Hedley's heart. He knew something was desperately wrong.

At school, Hedley couldn't keep his mind on his work. He kept on wondering what had happened. The street boy would never have left his dog all alone!

On the way home he stopped at the station. His parents had told him to always come directly home. But Hedley couldn't help himself.

The boy still wasn't there. And the dog looked so miserable on its own.

"Where's the boy who's always with that dog?" he asked the newspaperman.

"He's been taken ill," the man explained. "Gone to hospital, poor lad."

An awful feeling went through Hedley's body when he heard this.

"When's he coming back?"

"Dunno," the old man replied.

Hedley crossed the road and went indoors. He lay down on his bed, his head aching.

By the time his mother came home from work, he was weak and pale. She called for a doctor, who examined Hedley, then prescribed tablets.

Hedley's condition worsened during the night and he spent fitful hours tossing and turning, passing in and out of sleep, tortured by dreams of the street boy in hospital.

The whole of the next day, Hedley was feverish. At times he seemed to lose consciousness altogether. When he came round, he asked only for sips of water as the thought of food made him queasy. During the following night, his family were worried about him. He ranted and raved, complaining that they shouldn't have left him out in the snow in such freezing weather. He also didn't recognise his mother or father.

For three days Hedley was delirious. But on the morning of the fourth day, he woke up feeling very much better. The dizziness was gone, the nightmares had vanished, the fever had dropped.

He sat up, but he could hardly believe his eyes!

Where was he? He was shocked to find himself lying on a few sheets of cardboard, huddled inside a dark green sleeping bag.

He was outdoors!

He recognised the entrance to the boarded-up shop. Curled up beside him was a scruffy dog, which wagged its tail joyfully when it saw Hedley had woken up.

Hedley couldn't figure out what had happened. But here he was, dressed in clothes that were old and shabby, huddled in a sleeping bag, while people walked past without even noticing him.

"Morning, lad!"

It was the toothless newspaperman.

"You're looking a good deal better today," he added cheerfully.

"How did I get here?" Hedley asked.

"The same geyser who took you to hospital brought you back," the old man explained.

Hedley wanted to say he'd never been to hospital. But at that moment he noticed his father emerging from the house across the road.

He climbed out of his sleeping bag and rushed to greet him. The dog immediately followed. Hedley had to pick it up, so that they could cross the road safely. He had to wait for a break in the traffic and by the time Hedley reached his father, he was just getting into the car. Hedley's father deliberately pulled the car door shut and started the engine.

"Dad!" Hedley shouted.

Hedley's father barely looked at him as he drove off.

Hedley was stunned. His own father had not recognised him!

He marched up to the front door of his house and rang the doorbell.

His mother came to the door and opened it.

"What do you want?" she asked.

"Mum, don't you know who I am?" Hedley said.

Hedley's mother tried to shut the door, but Hedley put his foot out and prevented it from closing.

"Mum, it's me. Hedley!"

"Don't be ridiculous!" his mother said, looking at him with terror-stricken eyes. "Hedley's upstairs."

Hedley hardly knew what to say or do.

"Please let me in, Mum!"

"Go away!" she screamed. "Leave us alone or I'll call the police!"

Hedley backed away. His mother closed the door. He crossed the road back to the subway station. The dog snuggled up against him. He lay there, confused by the situation he found himself in.

A while later, Hedley noticed the curtains being opened in the upstairs room across the road.

A boy looked out of the window. Hedley recognised him. It was the street boy! In Hedley's room!

Hedley felt very strange. What was going on?

His stomach was growling with hunger.

"I'm starving," he said to the newspaperman.

"You've forgotten to put out your cap, lad," the old man responded. "But here, you can have this in the meantime."

The old man brought out half a sandwich from his pocket.

"Thanks," Hedley said.

Hedley found a cap under his sleeping bag and laid it out in front of him. The morning rush hour had started, but no one dropped any money into Hedley's cap.

The front door of the house across the street opened and the street boy emerged, dressed for school. He looked so clean! He walked past the station and disappeared around the corner.

The day passed slowly. Eventually, Hedley's cap contained a sprinkling of coins. He bought a packet of crisps from the station kiosk and shared it with the dog.

Later in the day, the street boy returned from school. Hedley saw him coming and ran forward to talk to him.

"Why are you living in my house?" Hedley asked.

The street boy looked at Hedley as if he was a dangerous madman.

"Leave me alone!" the boy said.

"No!" Hedley said firmly. "You stay here with your dog and give me the front door key so I can go home."

The street boy pulled away from Hedley, but Hedley grabbed hold of him and tried to feel for the key which he knew was in the boy's jacket pocket.

"Stop it!" the street boy shouted, defending himself.

The two boys started pulling at each other, punching and striking.

The newspaperman hobbled over and separated them.

"Enough of that, lads!"

The street boy straightened himself up and crossed the road.

"You shouldn't be allowed to live on the streets!" he yelled back, as he let himself in the front door.

That night Hedley slept outdoors. He huddled in his sleeping bag and hugged the dog for warmth. He thought of going to the police himself to tell them he was the real Hedley. But of course they wouldn't believe a boy dressed in shabby clothes.

Hedley found it difficult to sleep on the concrete. It was too cold, for one thing. And uncomfortable. And noisy. The cars going past made a terrific racket. Finally, when Hedley did fall asleep he was woken after just a few hours by some drunk men who were passing by. They had poured beer all over his sleeping bag just for a laugh. The men mocked Hedley and swore at him for a while before staggering off. Hedley didn't sleep much the rest of the night, as he was too damp.

The next morning, after the rush hour, Hedley was wondering how to get through the day, when suddenly he heard a voice.

"Oi!" the voice said. "Let's get to the food kitchen."

Hedley looked to see where the voice was coming from. The only thing nearby was the scruffy dog.

"Well, you comin' or what?"

It was the dog!

Hedley stashed his sleeping bag in a corner of the shop entrance.

"You can talk?" Hedley said.

"Well, no point going on about it," the dog said. "Let's get moving."

The dog knew the way. He had done this journey every day for months.

At the food kitchen, Hedley joined the queue of street people. All of them had spent their night somewhere on the streets. Some of them looked in really bad condition, coughing and spluttering. Others looked like ordinary folk, Hedley thought.

Inside the building Hedley downed a warm mug of tea and ate some beans on toast. It brought some life back to his aching body. One or two street people spoke to him, asked him where he hung out. But on the whole, he kept to himself.

After the meal, the dog said, "Oi, what about somfink for me then?"

So Hedley asked the person behind the counter if they had any scraps or leftovers.

"Here you are, Mutt," the woman said, offering the dog some cold chips and half a burger from the dustbin.

Hedley spent the rest of the day begging outside the station. In the afternoon, he spent what he had earned on a secondhand jumper he found in a charity shop.

One day followed after another. In a story, days can pass as quickly as this, but for Hedley each day was a day of real time.

Most people walked past him without a comment. Several of the older blokes in suits made nasty comments about boys begging for money from decent folks. But often young people stopped, spoke to him and gave him money. At nights he became accustomed to the noise of cars, but still he was woken by cats fighting, radios blasting out, or people arguing at three in the morning. One night he was woken by a torch shining into his face. It was the police! They searched his pockets, found nothing and told him he better find somewhere else to live soon.

The next day, Hedley was tired, bored and miserable.

"Oi, you need to look after yourself!" the dog said to him. "You're getting dirtier than me."

The dog led Hedley to a day centre where he was given a white dressing gown to change in to. He put the clothes he had worn for the last week into a washing machine. Then he went to shower.

Afterwards, Mutt said, "You smell a lot better now!"

All the time that he slept near the subway station, Hedley kept an eye on his old home. It was difficult for him to observe that family living their orderly lives, and the boy who used to live on the streets enjoying the warmth of Hedley's bedroom, while Hedley himself froze out there in the cold.

One evening Hedley noticed his father struggling to pull something large out of the back of his estate car. It was a shiny new bike! His father wheeled it to the front of the house and called the boy from upstairs to look at it. Hedley watched all this with interest. Then it dawned on him. It was his birthday! Of course it was! And Hedley's parents had told him they were going to buy him a bike.

Hedley watched as the other boy climbed on the bike. He seemed really pleased with the gift.

Hedley was furious.

He ran across the street and shouted at his parents.

"That bike's mine! It's my birthday today, not his! You're my parents!"

"Get out of here!" Hedley's father shouted. Then he told his wife to go indoors and call the police.

Hedley retreated back to his spot outside the boarded-up shop.

"Oi!" the dog said. "You've got us into trouble now."

Sure enough, later that evening the police arrived.

"You've got to move, son!" the constable said. "You can't sleep here any more. Find yourself a hostel."

"Can I just sleep here tonight?" Hedley asked. "I'll move in the morning."

"No," the constable answered. "You have to shift yourself now. We've had complaints."

Hedley picked up his sleeping bag. The police watched him as he disappeared down the street.

"Where to now?" Hedley wondered.

"I know another good doorway," the dog said. "Follow me! I used to hang out there before you found me."

Hedley followed the dog through the city, turning left, right, then straight on, past the city hall.

The dog led Hedley to a deep doorway, which was nicely sheltered from the cold rain and wind.

"Thanks, Mutt," Hedley said. "This place will do great."

He curled up in the corner nearest the shop door, held Mutt close to him, and thought about the night's events. Eventually, though, he fell asleep.

It was not long after that, though, when he felt himself being kicked!

"This is my bedroom!" someone was shouting. "You can't kip here."

Hedley sat up to find a furious chap hollering at him. He thought of putting up a fight, but the dog said, "Let's go! I know another place."

He led Hedley to an unoccupied doorway, which wasn't deep enough to keep out the rain. But it would do. Hedley covered his sleeping bag with a black dustbin liner to keep himself and Mutt dry.

The weeks passed. The months passed. In a story, months can pass as quickly as this, but for Hedley each month was a month of real time.

Hedley got to know some of the other street kids: Farrukh, who was a juggler; Donna, who was pregnant; Dave the Rave, who was into drugs.

Winter turned to spring, spring to summer, summer to autumn. In a story, a year can pass as quickly as this, but for Hedley the year was a year of real time. And after autumn, the cold wintry weather returned.

The first snow reminded Hedley of the subway station where he and the dog used to live.

"Let's go check it out, Mutt."

"Good idea," the dog replied.

Hedley and the dog approached the subway station. The shop was still boarded up. Hedley spoke to the toothless newspaperman.

"How you doin'?" Hedley asked.

"Not too bad," the old fellow answered.

"We're thinking of moving back here for a while," Hedley said. "What d'you reckon?"

"Try it," the old fellow suggested. "Perhaps they'll move you on again, I don't know."

"We got nothin' to lose," Hedley said.

So they moved in.

It was excellent to be back. Hedley kept watch on his old family again. His dad had a new car, he noticed. His little sister, Serena, now had a small three-wheeler bicycle of her own which she used in the garden. The street boy who had taken Hedley's place used his bike to cycle to school and back every day.

Late one afternoon, Hedley bumped into Dave the Rave. They greeted each other with a tap of the knuckles and stood talking on the pavement.

Out of the corner of his eye, Hedley noticed the boy from across the road, the one who lived in Hedley's bedroom, who slept in Hedley's bed, returning from school on the bike that should have been Hedley's.

Suddenly a car reversed out of a side-street without looking! An oncoming car had to swerve to avoid it. But now the swerving car was heading straight for the street boy on his bike!

Without hesitating, Hedley dived into the street and pulled the street boy out of the way. The bike and the two boys tumbled onto the pavement. But at least the car drove past without colliding into them or the bike.

The two boys lay on the tarmac. Hedley's head was aching! He had struck it on the pavement. Blood ran down the side of his face.

"Are you alright?"

Dave the Rave and the street boy were standing over him. They lifted him to his feet.

"Yeah, I'm not too bad."

"Take care next time!" the street boy said to him, passing him the bike. Some of the black covering had torn off the saddle, but otherwise the bike was in good shape.

Hedley was amazed to have the bike handed over to him!

What's going on? he thought.

The street boy and Dave the Rave walked off. The dog followed behind. Then the street boy and Dave the Rave parted company. Hedley watched in astonishment as the street boy returned to his spot at the subway station! He climbed into his green sleeping bag and the dog curled up beside him.

Hedley was dazed!

He thought that if the street boy had gone back to the subway station, perhaps he himself could try going back home.

So he did.

He wheeled his bike slowly across the road. He walked in through the gate of his house. His mother came running out of the front door.

"Hedley! Are you hurt?"

"No, I'm okay," Hedley answered.

"You've got blood on your face!" Serena said.

Hedley's mother fussed over his injury and led him indoors. He went upstairs to wash and change into other clothes. Then he went back into his bedroom. Everything was still the same. It was as if he had never been away!

How warm his bedroom was! And his bed seemed so soft and luxurious with its springy mattress and clean pillows. From the window he could see snow falling and the street boy huddled up in his green sleeping bag outside the boarded-up shop.

The street boy suddenly noticed Hedley looking at him. For a moment they stared at each other.

"It's going to be a cold winter for him," Hedley thought. "But I know what I'm going to do. I'm going to give him my old anorak to keep him warm."

And that's just what Hedley did.

Glass Room

Oh how sweet and innocent Janine was!

She lived in a house with her mother and stepfather. During the day they were an ordinary family. Janine went to school, her mother worked in a department store and her stepfather managed an office in the city.

On the weekends they were so kind to her, buying her as many sweets as she wanted. Anyone seeing them together in the park or at the shopping centre or on the beach might have thought they were the happiest family in the world.

But Janine lived in a house with a secret room, a room with glass walls. That room was secret from the world outside. No one in the whole wide world knew about that room except for Janine and her mother and stepfather. From that room you could not see out, but from Janine's room, she could see in.

And what things she saw each night!

Janine saw the magician, the wicked magician, with a black moustache and dressed in his smart black suit, top-hat, bow-tie and white gloves, pulling a shining, silvery sword from the air. She saw his assistant, the beautiful Cosmo, dressed in sparkling tights, high-heel shoes and a starry, sequinned, tight-fitting pink jacket, twirling around in time to the music that was playing.

"Who is tonight's little volunteer?" the magician asked.

"Tonight it's this pretty girl with the blue eyes," the assistant would answer, lifting a veil from the girl who trembled with fear.

She was wearing a sleeveless white dress, her hair braided with bows, her cheeks reddened with stage make-up.

"And what's your name, my dear?" the magician asked.

"C... C... Carolette," the girl stammered.

"Carolette, what a lovely name," the wicked magician said, twisting his black moustache. "Thank you, Cosmo. You may go now. Come back when I ring my golden bell!"

The beautiful Cosmo pirouetted out of the glass room and closed the door behind her.

"Now, Carolette," the magician said. "Let's lay you in this box."

He helped Carolette to climb into a long black box.

"Now I'll close the lid," he said. "You're not afraid of the dark are you, my dear?"

Janine watched as the wicked magician raised his shining, silvery sword above his head.

"Watch carefully now," the magician said, "as I perform a trick rarely seen. I will cut the lovely Carolette into small pieces."

The wicked magician brought down the sword sharply and cut through the box that Carolette was lying in.

"Look," he said. "The box is now in two pieces."

He pulled the two pieces of the box apart to show that they really were not joined.

"Watch carefully," he said, as he brought the sword down again and again and again.

The long black box was now in five pieces, each small enough for the magician to lift into the air and hold as he marched around in time to the music.

"Here is one leg," he said, holding up one small piece of the box, and sure enough there was Carolette's lovely leg.

"And here is the other," he said, and sure enough there it was.

"And here is one arm," he said, and sure enough there was Carolette's lovely arm.

"And here is the other," he said, and sure enough there it was.

"And finally," he said, "here is Carolette's head."

He lifted the piece of the box high above his head, turned around twice, then opened it to reveal Carolette's head.

Carolette's mouth was still talking!

"Please," she whimpered, "don't hurt me!"

"I won't hurt you, my dear," the wicked magician said. "In fact, I'm going to put you all together again, good as new."

He threw his sword up into the air and it vanished in a puff of smoke.

Then he pulled a magic wand from the air.

"Now, as I utter the magic words, Carolette's arms and legs and head will join together. Just watch carefully."

The magician concentrated on the five pieces of the box which lay before him.

He pushed these pieces together until they all touched each other.

"Al jehurra kenassi beshurra kedal!" the wicked magician chanted.

He lifted the lid and Carolette sat up.

"Are you all in one piece?" the magician asked.

Carolette stepped out of the box.

"Good. I'm sure you enjoyed that," the magician said. "But you must never tell anyone in the whole wide world what went on here tonight, because this is the most secret magic there is."

Then the magician picked up the golden bell and rang it loud and clear.

Cosmo, the assistant, came dancing in through the door of the glass room.

"The show is over for tonight," the magician announced. "Well done, Carolette. Do a curtsy!"

And Carolette had to curtsy. The magician and

Cosmo clapped their hands.

"You can take Carolette back now," the magician said to his assistant.

Cosmo wrapped the veil around Carolette and led her out of the glass room.

Night after night Janine watched the magic show. It made her flesh creep to see the wicked magician cut up the lovely Carolette into five pieces.

"One day," she told herself, "I'm going to rescue that Carolette from the wicked magician."

But she couldn't think how to do it.

The show was always the same, night after night, the sweet Carolette chopped into five pieces and then put back again. Always the same costumes, always the same music, always the same magic chant, "Al jehurra kenassi beshurra kedal!"

Until one night, the wicked magician chopped the black box into five pieces and when he showed what was in each piece – the two arms, the two legs, the head of Carolette with the mouth whimpering, "Please don't hurt me!" – each of the pieces was bleeding!

Red blood smeared all over the sweet Carolette's arms and legs and head!

Janine couldn't bear it! She screamed and screamed and screamed!

Then the wicked magician pushed the pieces of the box together. He chanted, "Al jehurra kenassi beshurra kedal!" And Carolette sat up as good as new, all in one piece, and sparkling clean. No trace of blood anywhere!

"Wasn't that the most brilliant magical trick you've ever seen?" the wicked magician asked.

He rang the golden bell and when Cosmo, the assistant, came into the glass room, she and the magician clapped and shouted, "Bravo! Bravo!"

But that night, after the show, Janine couldn't sleep a wink. Next morning, when she got to school, she couldn't sit still in class, so she ran out of the classroom into the playground. Beyond the playground was the woods leading down to the footpath. It was forbidden to go beyond the playground into those woods.

But Janine opened the gate and ran through. Tears were streaming down her face. She ran into the middle of the woods, on and on, not caring where she was heading. And then she stopped and leaned against the trunk of an old tree.

She wept and wept, and then she blurted out the secret she was never supposed to tell anyone in the whole wide world.

"The wicked magician made Carolette bleed!" she screamed. "The wicked magician chopped Carolette into five pieces and made her bleed!"

Unseen by Janine, a glistening black raven sitting at the top of the tree, heard her words.

Immediately it flew off over the woods screeching, "The wicked magician made Carolette bleed!"

Towards the school it flew, screeching, "The wicked magician chopped Carolette into five pieces and made her bleed!"

Janine slumped down to the bottom of the trunk

and sobbed. She wished she didn't ever have to go back home. She wished she could disappear from the world. She wished she could forget everything that had happened night after night.

Suddenly, Janine felt hands on her shoulders. They were gently trying to comfort her.

"Janine? Janine? Are you alright?"

It was her teacher, Miss Gresham.

Janine sobbed uncontrollably.

"My poor dear," Miss Gresham said soothingly, "we must do something about that wicked magician. I know someone who can help."

That night, just as the show in the glass room was about to begin – Cosmo, the assistant, was twirling around in her sequinned jacket, and the wicked magician was pulling his shining, silvery sword from the air – just then, while Carolette stood trembling under her veil, there was an urgent banging on the door. Then a noise of wood shattering.

White smoke filled the glass room followed by a flash of brilliant light. Out of nowhere, there before them stood a white-bearded wizard, holding a staff which was crackling with little flames.

"I am the Great Marquez!" he announced. "One move, and you will be sizzled to ashes!"

The wicked magician and Cosmo, the assistant, looked petrified.

Carolette shuffled closer to the Great Marquez.

"I have come to put an end to this show!" he said in his great booming voice. He stared at the wicked magician so fiercely that the magician had to turn his head away. "Never again will you perform your wicked magic!"

The Great Marquez banged three times on the floor with his staff. And each time a flash of lightning blinded everyone in the room.

Then the Great Marquez stepped across to the wicked magician, grabbed hold of his shining, silvery sword and broke it in half. (It was only made of cardboard.) He put the golden bell on the floor and stamped it flat so that it could never ring again. He pulled off the wicked magician's top-hat, bow-tie and gloves, squeezing them until they turned to ashes. Then the Great Marquez ripped off the wicked magician's moustache! The wicked magician slumped to the floor.

And suddenly the wicked magician didn't look like a magician any longer. He looked like Janine's stepfather!

The Great Marquez turned to Cosmo, the assistant, and banged again three times on the floor with his staff. Again the lightning flashed. This time a dressing gown appeared in his hands, which he wrapped around Cosmo.

And suddenly, she didn't look like a wicked magician's assistant any longer. She looked like Janine's mother! And she was sobbing, crying, "I'm so sorry! I'm so sorry!"

Finally, the Great Marquez turned to Carolette. Once more he banged on the floor three times with his staff. Lightning flashed in all directions.

He took a handkerchief from his pocket and

wiped the red stage make-up from her face.

Suddenly she didn't look like Carolette any longer. She looked like Janine!

"Never again will you have to pretend to be Carolette," he said tenderly to her.

Then the Great Marquez faced Janine's step-father. "Your wicked magic has come to an end," he boomed. "The show is over. This glass room is secret no longer."

He banged three times on the floor with his staff. The glass windows of the little room immediately began to melt. They melted into pools of liquid on the floor, which then evaporated into wisps of steam.

Nothing was left of the secret room.

"And now," the Great Marquez said, "I give to this girl Janine the gift of sleep during the night and during the day the power to grow and to understand herself and others. She will see her parents for who they truly are. And from this day forth I will be watching over her to keep her safe."

You Must
You Must
You Must

SPELLBREAKER
FRIDA FROTH

If you've heard this story before, then you've heard more than I have, because I've never heard it before and I've heard most stories.

It happened in a city which was pretty much like any other city, except that everything painted blue in other cities was painted red. And it happened in a time exactly like now. Except that it was then.

In this city there lived a girl called Megan. A bonny and cheerful lass she was, with hair the colour of milk chocolate and a smile that lit up the neighbourhood.

Now this Megan was approaching a very marriageable age. Young lads swarmed around, barking like wild dogs.

"Megan, please marry me!" one would say, showing off the mountainous muscles on his upper arms.

"No, marry me!" insisted another, inviting her into his gleaming sports car.

"It would be a great mistake to marry anyone other than myself!" said a third, combing his grease-black hair and posing like a film-star.

But Megan would have none of them, until one day a soft-spoken young man named Conrad Avery was introduced to her at a disco.

How interesting Conrad seemed to her and how easily they spoke together, talking about this and about that. He was gentle, Conrad was, a little nervous maybe, but he became more confident as his affection towards Megan blossomed into love.

In due course, he showed Megan a photograph of his family, a photograph he kept in his wallet at all times. How tenderly he spoke of his parents, his grandparents and his great-aunt. It made Megan feel warm towards Conrad to think how much of a family man he was.

"He is the very one for me," Megan thought to herself. "He loves me and I love him. He will make a caring father to my children."

When, after some months, he proposed marriage, she accepted.

But the day after her wedding, Megan was in for a big surprise.

It happened like this.

They woke up in the morning and Conrad said, "Good morning dear wife! An apple a day keeps the doctor away!"

"Good morning dear husband," she said. "What's this about apples?"

"Don't you know," he replied, "that when we wake up you must say 'An apple a day keeps the doctor away!' otherwise the day won't go well."

"Very well," she laughed. "An apple a day keeps the doctor away!"

Conrad washed and dressed, then helped cook the breakfast but before sitting down, he placed the newspaper on top of his head, and said, "Merrily we roll along."

"What's this merrily we roll along business?" his wife asked.

"Don't you know," her husband replied, "that before eating you must always do this otherwise the food will taste like cow dung?"

"Very well," Megan laughed. And she placed a newspaper on her head and said, "Merrily we roll along."

After breakfast they both put on their coats and walked to the car to drive to work.

But before he climbed in, Conrad walked around the car three times, and each time he said, "May the heavens swallow up all fishcrabs!"

"What's all this?" Megan asked.

"Don't you know," Conrad said, "that you must do this before climbing into a car, otherwise you will never reach your destination."

"Is this really necessary?" Megan asked.

"Indeed it is!" Conrad said. "Please, Megan, otherwise I'll never get to work safely!"

Out of love for her husband Megan circled the car three times and each time she repeated, "May the heavens swallow up all fishcrabs!"

That evening, when he finished his work at the post office, Conrad collected his wife from the bank where she worked. He pecked her sweetly on the cheek and they drove home like any two newly-weds in love, glad to be together.

Conrad parked the car in the driveway, then used his key to open the front door. He stepped into the house with his right foot, then stepped out of it with his left, three times in a row, each time accompanying the action with the words "Toosh-aloosh." Only when this was completed correctly did he go indoors.

"What's this toosh-aloosh business?" Megan asked.

"Don't you know," Conrad replied, "that you must say 'Toosh-aloosh' before entering a house otherwise there will be no happiness in the home."

So Megan said "Toosh-aloosh" while stepping in and out of the house three times.

After dinner, before he could do the washing up, Conrad touched the taps, counting to 21. But he didn't count in the usual way. What he did was this, "1, 2, 3 ... 2, 3, 4 ... 3, 4, 5 ... 4, 5, 6 ... " and so on, so that it took a great deal longer than it would have if he simply counted in the ordinary way.

"What's all this counting for?" Megan asked.

"Don't you know," Conrad replied, "that if you don't count to 21 in this precise way, your children will never grow up healthy, wealthy and wise?"

So Megan was forced to touch the taps and count.

"1, 2, 3 ..." she said. "2, 3, 4 ... 3, 4, 5 ... 4, 5, 6 ..." all the way up to 21.

After washing up they spent several delightful hours in each other's company. Megan really was very fond of Conrad and he was equally fond of her.

When it was time to go to sleep, Conrad brushed his teeth, changed into his pyjamas, then climbed into bed.

After a brief silence, he curled into a small ball and mumbled, "Sheep in the meadow, cows in the corn."

Then he straightened himself out and smiled at her.

"What's this sheep and cow business?" she asked him.

"Don't you know," he said, "that the stars will fall on our house unless we say this?"

So Megan curled herself into a small ball and mumbled, "Sheep in the meadow, cows in the corn."

Then she straightened herself and kissed her husband goodnight.

The next morning when Megan awoke, she thought of pleasing Conrad, so she turned to him and said, "Good morning dear husband! An apple a day keeps the doctor away!"

Conrad jumped out of bed, fretting and fuming. He went into the bathroom and washed his hands twenty-four times, each time repeating, "Forget the walruses! Forgive the warthogs!"

"What did I do wrong?" she asked anxiously.

"Don't you know," he said, "that today is Tuesday? On Tuesdays you must say 'An orange a day keeps the dentist away!'"

Poor Megan!

She soon learned that everything was slightly different on a Tuesday, different again on Wednesday, Thursday, Friday, and utterly different on Saturday and Sunday!

It took her ages to learn all the words and actions for each different occasion.

But that was just the tip of the iceberg!

Over the next few months, Megan learned that Conrad only made her perform the most necessary actions. There were hundreds of others, less important, that Conrad himself was compelled to perform: tying shoelaces, going to the toilet, opening cupboards, feeding the cat – all these had to be repeated until done correctly, with the appropriate words, otherwise Conrad felt things would not go well for him or his wife. And on the first day of each month all these had to be done backwards!

But Megan loved Conrad, so she tried her best to help her husband through each day.

After a year though, she noticed that other actions were being added to the list. And the actions were becoming more and more complicated! For example, after dinner, they had to count to larger and larger numbers, first to thirty-one, forty-one, fifty-one, then right up to one hundred and one! "1, 2, 3 ... 2, 3, 4 ... 3, 4, 5 ... 4, 5, 6 ..." all the way up to one hundred and one!

One day they were out shopping at the supermarket. They had bought everything they needed and Conrad took out his wallet to pay for the goods. When he received the receipt, he jumped up and down three times and said, "Forever's a long time to fill with pigeons!"

He pushed the trolley out the revolving doors. As they neared the car, he stopped, put his fingers in his ears and shouted, "Gateway to the stars!"

Megan was so embarrassed! It was the first time Conrad had acted like this in public. But Megan simply held his hand and reassured him. "It's alright darling," she said.

Later, after they had packed the boxes into the car, Megan wheeled the trolley back to the trolley-park.

Suddenly she felt a tap on her shoulder. She turned around to see a most unusual person. He was short and plump with a purple face, a long yellow beard, curly yellow hair and enormous feet.

"Excuse me, lady," he said. "But I couldn't help noticing your husband earlier ..."

"It's none of your business," she said.

"That's true," the man answered. "But I may be able to help..."

"How can you...?"

"Your husband's under a spell," the man continued, "and I'm a Nonnigon."

"What's that?" Megan asked.

"Nonnigons are brilliant spell-breakers," he explained.

The man fished in his pocket and pulled out a small business card.

"If you ever need me, give me a call."

And with that the man was gone, flapping his overlarge feet as he walked off.

Megan looked at the card. There, in gold letters, were printed the words: SPELLBREAKER FRIDAFROTH. But the rest of the card, including the back, was blank. There was no number to call!

"That's not much use!" Megan thought to herself, slipping the card into her purse.

In time, she forgot about the card, but she did begin to wonder if her husband was indeed under a spell. Every minute of every day was taken up with tiresome actions. There was hardly a moment for anything else! And how complicated all the actions were. After dinner now, they both had to touch the taps counting to five hundred and one! It took ever so long! "1, 2, 3 ... 2, 3, 4 ... 3, 4, 5 ... 4, 5, 6 ..." all the way up to five hundred and one!

After two years of marriage, Megan was becoming increasingly unhappy. It was distressing to watch her husband's life – and her own – being swallowed up by all these actions. But what bothered her more than anything else was the fact that she wanted to have a baby. How could she with all this going on?

"If I ever had a child," she thought, "it would also have to live under this terrible spell. It would have to learn all these words and actions! Never, never, never!"

She went upstairs to her bedroom, shut the door and wept and wept.

"Oh, if only that Nonnigon had left me his number," she thought to herself. "Perhaps he might have been able to break the spell."

She searched her purse for the card. There it was: SPELLBREAKER FRIDAFROTH.

What could she do to find him? Tears rolled down her cheeks and dripped onto the blank card.

To her astonishment, letters began to form where the tears fell. Vague yellow letters, but visible enough. Now the card read: NEED HELP? CALL 78445920.

Megan picked up the telephone and dialled.

"Institute of Spell-breaking," the voice on the other end answered. "Yes, you can have an appointment with Fridafroth but there's a long waiting list. The earliest appointment is in three months time." The voice gave her a time and date.

Later in the day, Megan told Conrad about the phone call. But he didn't want to hear about it. He didn't want to keep the appointment. He agreed he might be under a spell, but if he went to a spell-breaker, he might have to stop doing these things. Then something bad might happen to them!

Megan, however, was insistent. If he loved her, she said, he'd come with her to the spell-breaker.

"Alright," he agreed. "But don't expect me to change my ways!"

The weeks passed and as the day of the appointment approached, Conrad became increasingly nervous. But he didn't want to disappoint Megan.

The Institute of Spell-breaking was in a recently constructed part of the city which they had never seen before. The buildings were all of unusual shapes and colours. Megan and Conrad eventually located the Institute itself, a curved building with an imposing entrance flanked by tall pillars.

"I can't go in there!" Conrad screamed. "I can't, Megan! I'm sorry, I just can't!"

He turned to the left and ran down the street as fast as he could. But he didn't get that far, because the road ended abruptly at the river, where a large ferry boat, loaded with cars and passengers, was heading out to sea.

Megan walked in the direction Conrad had gone and found him at the river's edge, in a state of panic.

"Forget the worms! Forgive the woodpeckers!"

"Dear Conrad," she said tenderly. "Put your hand here!" She placed Conrad's hand on her stomach.

"What is it?" he asked her.

"Can't you feel?" she said. "Can't you feel any kicking?"

Conrad's hand felt little movements coming from inside Megan's tummy.

"It's our baby, Conrad," Megan said. "I'm pregnant!"

Conrad stared at her. Gradually he calmed down and began to smile as a feeling of joy came over him.

"I'm going to be a father!" he yelped, clapping his hands and jumping around.

"Yes, Conrad. And you can do something right now for your baby. You can come and see the spell-breaker."

"Yes, dear. Of course."

Arm in arm, Conrad and Megan entered the Institute. The interior of the building was sparsely furnished. They had to cross a broad expanse of floor to reach the reception counter.

"Yes, who have we here?"

The words issued from a short and plump, yellow-bearded, curly-haired Nonnigon, sitting on a tall stool. He asked for their names and particulars.

"Fridafroth will see you shortly," the receptionist said. "Please take a seat."

They sat anxiously in the waiting area. From time to time various Nonnigons scurried from one side of the building to the other, their large feet flapping the floor with each step.

After a long wait, Megan recognised the one coming towards them.

"Mrs Avery, how good to see you again. And you, sir," he said, extending a hand towards Conrad. "I apologise for keeping you waiting. Busy day. People under such stresses and strains nowadays. Spellbound in more ways than you can possibly imagine."

He led them into his consulting room, which was furnished with a desk, three chairs and floor-to-ceiling shelves laden with numerous bottles and books. There were also several pot-plants scattered around the room, some of them with spiky stems, hairy leaves and bell-like blooms.

"Take a seat please."

Nonnigon Fridafroth spent an hour talking to Megan and Conrad, learning about each word and action that they were compelled to repeat during any one day.

"Aha, an orange a day..." he said, gazing at them over his spectacles. "Oho, toosh-aloosh... Mmmhmm, walruses and warthogs... I think I'm getting the picture."

"Can you help us, Mr Fridafroth?" Megan asked.

"Only with your co-operation, Mr Avery."

"Certainly, Mr Fridafroth."

"Please stand in front of the mirror."

Neither Conrad nor Megan had noticed the full-length mirror until then. They had never seen one like it before. It was made of black glass.

"Now, who do you see in that mirror? Look closely, Mr Avery."

Conrad stared at his image.

"It's me, of course," he replied.

"Keep looking!" Nonnigan Fridafroth insisted. "Don't turn away."

Conrad fixated his gaze on the mirror.

"Good heavens!" he exclaimed suddenly. "That's my great-aunt staring back at me!"

"Your great-aunt!" Nonnigon Fridaforth repeated. "So, it was she who cast the spell!"

Conrad was bewildered.

"You can sit down now, Mr Avery."

Megan patted Conrad's arm gently.

"What we need to do now," Nonnigon Fridafroth

continued, "is to break the power she has over you."

"How can we do that?" Conrad asked.

"Can you tell me more about her? Describe her to me," Nonnigon Fridafroth said.

"She was …. She was …" Conrad tried to think of what to say.

"Show your photograph," Megan suggested.

"Which photograph is that?" Nonnigon Fridafroth asked.

"He keeps a family photograph in his wallet," Megan explained.

"May I see it!" Nonnigon Fridafroth requested, holding out his hand.

Conrad anxiously took the photo from the wallet.

"No!" he exclaimed, clutching the photo tightly. "I have never let anyone else hold it."

Megan turned sweetly to her husband, who furrowed his brow and scowled.

"Come now, dear," she implored.

"Forget the wolves! Forgive the weasels!" Conrad cried, as he placed the photograph in the Nonnigon's hands. "My great aunt is the one in the top corner of the picture."

Nonnigon Fridafroth examined the photograph closely.

Then, suddenly, he pointed at Conrad's left hand.

"Whose ring is that?" he asked, pointing at the broad gold band on Conrad's fourth finger.

"It's mine!" Conrad said.

"Yes, but who gave it to you?"

"Somebody when I was twelve..." Conrad said.

"Yes, yes," Nonnigon Fridafroth said. "But who was it that gave it to you?"

Conrad pursed his lips and looked around as if he were searching for a way out.

"My... my... my great-aunt!"

"Conrad," Megan said gently. "I never knew that."

"Give it to me!" Nonnigon Fridafroth said.

"I can't," Conrad answered.

"Why not?"

"Because it doesn't come off my finger."

Conrad pulled on it to show how the ring refused to budge. His finger was much plumper now than when he first put it on all those years ago.

Nonnigon Fridafroth rose from his chair and consulted a book which was so thick it weighed more than himself.

"Aha... oho... mmmhmmm..." he muttered, as he browsed through the information contained in those weighty pages.

Then he started pouring substances from bottles into a glass beaker which he heated on a gas burner. It gurgled and gargled! He plucked a crimson flower from one of the pot-plants near his desk, then carefully tore it into small pieces which he added to the brew. It sputtered and spattered! A thick crimson smoke rose up to the ceiling and a powerful odour pervaded the room. Finally, he took the photograph of Conrad's family and held the top corner of it in the crimson smoke with a long pair of tweezers.

Conrad broke into a dreadful sobbing.

"Forget the wasps! Forgive the weevils!"

"There, there, my dear," Megan said, comforting her husband with an arm around his shoulders.

After a while, Nonnigon Fridafroth returned the photograph to Conrad.

"I have treated it with spell-breaking vapours," he explained. "Now the ring will come off easily."

Conrad pulled on the ring, and it slid off without any difficulty.

"You can keep the photograph," the Nonnigon said. "But you need to be freed from the power of this ring."

He walked across to the gas burner and dropped the gold ring into the sizzling mixture.

It fizzed and whizzed, slowly dissolving until it was no thicker than a fine wire. Then it broke in two, dissolved further until it completely vanished.

Conrad broke into a dreadful sobbing.

"Forget the weasels! Forgive the wombats!"

Nonnigon Fridafroth continued his brewing. He allowed the mixture to boil for a while, after which he poured the crimson liquid into a large bottle.

"Now, Mr Avery, what I'd like you to do is to think of one your rituals and write the words that you say on this piece of paper. Choose carefully which you'd like to get rid of first."

Conrad thought for a moment, then wrote, "An apple a day keeps the doctor away."

"Very good," Mr Avery. "Now I'd like you to drop the piece of paper in the bottle."

Conrad did as he was asked. The liquid sizzled and sozzled. Crimson vapours issued from the bottle as the piece of paper dissolved and disappeared entirely.

"Excellent! Excellent! I don't think that one will give you any trouble tomorrow," Nonnigon Fridafroth exclaimed. "I would like you to take this bottle home with you. Each day, write the words of a different ritual on a piece of paper and drop it in. Every time you do that it will make the spell weaker. After a few months, you'll be much happier and the power of the spell will be broken forever."

"Thank you very much, Mr Fridafroth," Megan said, as she and her husband took their bottle and left.

"My pleasure, my pleasure!" the Nonnigon said, waving them goodbye.

The following morning Conrad awoke and did not mention any fruit. Instead, he turned to Megan and said, "Good morning dear wife! I have a feeling this day is going to go very well."

Megan was overjoyed.

"Why don't you sizzle another one of your rituals right now?"

Conrad agreed. He wrote "Merrily we roll along" on a piece of paper and dropped it into the bottle. Again, crimson vapours spiralled from the bottle as the piece of paper dissolved and disappeared entirely.

When he sat down to breakfast he did not put the newspaper on his head, nor did the food taste like cow dung.

"This breakfast is delicious!" he said to Megan.

The following day, Conrad sizzled the words "May the heavens swallow up all fishcrabs." When it was time to go to work, he did not mention fishcrabs nor did he walk around the car three times. He and Megan climbed into the car, drove off and reached their destinations safely.

Oh what relief Megan and Conrad felt! It was as if a huge and heavy metal coat had been removed from each of them and they could now move freely, stretching their arms and dancing to the happy music of their lives.

Some months later, a lovely baby daughter was born to the happy couple. What proud parents they were! And the baby grew up free from the spell which had blighted her father.

You may be wondering if Conrad was totally freed from his spell? The answer, I'm pleased to tell you, is … yes. Except for one thing. Every 29th day of February, Conrad would greet his wife first thing in the morning with "A peach a day keeps the nurse away!"

As that only occurred once every four years, it didn't cause too much of a problem!

Satanium

Barnaby Gribb was the most famous scientist of his generation, though to most people who knew him in his early days, he looked perfectly ordinary. If you could have seen him in a supermarket your first thought would not have been, "There's a brilliant scientist!" He didn't wear a white lab-coat, he didn't have wild white hair, and he didn't wear thick-lensed glasses.

In fact, most people who knew him thought of him in a favourable light. They could never have guessed what would befall him.

First we have to realise that Barnaby was very, very, very, very intelligent. Please note, that's four 'verys'. Three 'verys' wouldn't adequately describe him at all. When it came to intelligence, Barnaby

was definitely a 'four-very' man. He had been a
Professor of Astrobiophysicology at the University
since the age of thirteen, though he was only
required to teach there one day each year. The rest
of the time he spent in the laboratory, which he had
built at great expense on the very summit of the
tallest hill in the city.

He had once been married to a beautiful chemist
he met at a scientific conference. But after giving
birth to a baby daughter, his young wife fell in love
with a pop-star and flew off with him to California.
Barnaby was left with the baby, Kaylie, whom he
loved just about more than anything else in the
world. He hired a nanny to take care of her while he
was busy doing his research (which was most of the
time, it has to be said).

Barnaby allowed himself three tea-breaks per day
– at eleven o'clock in the morning, four o'clock in
the afternoon, and nine o'clock at night. His assistant, a snazzily dressed young man called John
Feather, served him Earl Grey tea in the laboratory.
During these tea-breaks, Barnaby loved to sit in
his old wicker chair, sipping the hot drink and
randomly solving any problems which occurred to
him.

It was at these moments that he made some of his
most remarkable breakthroughs, like finding the
first black hole in England, which everyone now
knows is in Ipswich, and the discovery of "nizzles",
those microscopic creatures which cause people to
sneeze exactly when they do.

Kaylie in the meantime grew into a charming young girl. She was proud of her father, though during the week she only saw him at mealtimes, and at bedtimes when he would read her a scientific article to help her fall asleep. At weekends, however, they had good times together and Barnaby was grateful to have the company of such a sweet daughter.

Perhaps their happiness would have continued had it not been for Barnaby's overwhelming desire to become the most famous scientist of all. It was this ambition which led him deeper and deeper into forbidden areas of research. It was his belief that the human brain used only ten per cent of its potential. He therefore began to experiment with the components of life-energy itself, in the hope of producing a substance which would reach that part of the brain which other substances failed to reach.

Day after day, year after year, Barnaby experimented with various potions that increased intelligence or mental power, prevented the onset of baldness, or enabled humans to live longer. His laboratory filled with an alarming collection of fungi, sea-creatures and the internal organs of seals, orang-utans and turtles.

The closer he came to his goal, the more excited Barnaby became.

One morning, during his tea-break, he exploded with joy.

"My dear Feather!" he exclaimed. "I believe I have done it! A substance which will give me superhuman powers and everlasting fame!"

During his afternoon tea-break, Barnaby worked out most of the formula. During the evening tea-break, he almost solved the problem of how to manufacture the product.

I can't reveal to you the exact ingredients in Professor Gribb's formula, for fear that you might try to produce it yourself and then the awful things that happened to the professor might happen to you. But I can tell you it involved the skins of certain frogs, the horn of a rhinoceros, nitroglycerine, cobra venom, the liver of a shark, the juice of a nettle, and the tail of a rat.

But there was still something lacking in his formula. As he sat in his old wicker chair late that night, he felt uneasy.

"It needs an extra something," he said to himself as he dozed off for a few moments. "Something particularly potent..."

"Perhaps I can help you," he heard a voice utter.

The professor sat up in a state of dazed surprise! There, on the end of his desk, wrapped in a mantle of flames, perched a small fellow. His eyes were completely white and his ears resembled bat's wings. His skin consisted of thousands of tiny scales like a fish and his hands and feet were clawed like a bird's.

"Who are you?" the professor asked.

"Why, surely you recognise me?" the little fellow said. "I've been your inspiration all these years. The one who has given you all your best ideas."

"Oh yes," Barnaby said. "I've just never met you in person before."

"Well, I thought I'd better come in the flesh, so to speak, because you need a little inspiration tonight."

"That's true," Professor Gribb said. "I just can't figure out the missing ingredient."

"That's because you're thinking you need something potent," the little fellow said, "whereas in truth you need something pure and innocent."

"Pure and innocent? What are you talking about?"

"I'm talking about something soft and golden."

"Soft and golden? Can't you be more specific?"

"Yes, Professor, I can. I'm referring to your daughter's hair."

"Kaylie's hair?"

"Yes," the little fellow explained. "Her hair is the missing ingredient."

"Oh, well, she won't miss one or two hairs from her head."

"That wouldn't be enough."

"A lock of hair, then. Will that do?"

"No way! What is required is all her hair!"

"All of it!" Barnaby cried out. "But then she'll be bald!"

"Bald as an egg, Professor. But you'll go down in history as the inventor of the most powerful substance ever known on earth, mark my words!"

Barnaby Gribb pondered the situation.

"Oh, alright!" he said. "It will all grow back in time, I expect."

The little fellow beamed.

"You're a true man of science, Professor Gribb. And I wish you the success you deserve."

The creature hopped off the bed and flew towards the open window.

"It's been a pleasure, Professor Gribb."

And with that he soared off into the night sky, his mantle of flames glowing fainter and fainter in the distance.

Barnaby roused himself from his bed. Armed with a large pair of scissors he entered his daughter's bedroom. How sweetly she slept!

Barnaby raised the scissors to his daughter's hair.

"No, I can't do it!" he said. "I can't, I can't, I can't, I can't, I can't, I can't... I can!"

And he snipped off every hair from his daughter's head!

He rushed back to his laboratory with an armful of soft, flowing locks.

He threw his daughter's hair into a canister of boiling black syrup. It bubbled up into a golden froth.

Professor Gribb worked all night. It was still boiling in the morning when John Feather turned up for work.

"Am I not the cleverest man on earth, Mr Feather? And is this not my greatest achievement?"

John Feather helped Professor Gribb add the remainder of the ingredients. The liquid was then passed through spiral tubes into thick-walled chambers where laser-beams flashed violet and green. After this, it was blended in a revolving tub which looked much like a washing machine.

"I have decided to call this substance 'satanium'," Barnaby announced, "in honour of a little visitor I had last night."

"A fine name!" John Feather agreed.

It was at this moment that Kaylie came rushing into the laboratory, weeping miserably.

"Daddy, Daddy!" she cried. "Look what happened to me during the night!"

"Oh you poor thing!" Professor Gribb said soothingly, hugging her close. "You're as bald as an egg! But don't worry, I still love you."

"But how did it happen, Daddy?"

"I've no idea!" Professor Gribb said, lying through his teeth. "But hurry up, now, or you'll be late for school."

"I can't go to school like this!" Kaylie sobbed. "Everyone will laugh at me."

"Oh, very well, then," Barnaby said. "Take a few days off until it grows back."

Kaylie ran back to her room, wailing at the disaster which had befallen her.

That very afternoon, the first drops of satanium were finally distilled into a small test-tube. It was a victorious moment for Barnaby Gribb.

"Professor, you are a genius!" John Feather said, congratulating him with a vigorous handshake.

"I completely agree with you, Mr Feather," Professor Gribb replied.

When enough satanium had been produced to fill the test-tube, it was plugged with a leak-proof cork which the professor had specially invented. The professor held it up to the light. The liquid was almost transparent, but tinged with gold.

"Beautiful!" he exclaimed.

The satanium tests were conducted scientifically. John Feather had to swear an oath to Professor Gribb that he would never, under any circumstances, divulge any of the results to the world outside. First they tried it on a model aeroplane. One drop of satanium was placed in its fuel tank.

"Here we go!" Professor Gribb shouted.

He launched the plane and it soared up into the air. Within seconds it disappeared from sight.

"Wow!" John Feather exclaimed. "That's power alright!"

A week later the model plane was recovered in Antarctica where a scientist observed it running out of energy and floating down to a perfect landing on the ice.

"What do you think of that, Mr Feather?" Professor Gribb asked his assistant.

"It's immense," the assistant replied.

"Tomorrow we'll try it on the cat!" Professor Gribb announced.

The cat was Jessica, an old Siamese who slept twenty-three hours out of every twenty-four. She only awoke to eat and drink and do her business.

One drop of satanium was placed on Jessica's tongue. She leaped into the air, her hair standing on end, her tail straight up, her eyes bulging and glowing orange, a vicious mewling issuing from her mouth. She bounded across the laboratory, out through a window, across the garden and headed straight for the professor's huge Alsatian. Claws outstretched, she flew like a missile at the dog's face, as if she were wreaking the vengeance of all cats on all dogs. The Alsatian fled for its life, howling in agony. Next, Jessica dashed through the garden gate out into the fields beyond. From the laboratory window, Professor Gribb and John Feather watched in amazement as the revitalised cat sped through the long grass and disappeared into the distance.

That evening, the newspapers were full of stories of a wild beast that had attacked chickens, geese, sheep and apparently even babies in their buggies. It was past midnight before Jessica returned to Professor Gribb's house. She sidled in and fell asleep in her usual place on the arm of the settee, just as if nothing unusual had happened to her all day. She slept most of the day, only waking up to eat and use the sand-tray.

"Now," Professor Gribb announced, "it is time to test the satanium on myself!"

"Are you sure?" John Feather asked.

"I have never been more certain of anything in my life!"

The professor asked his assistant to make notes of everything he did while under the influence of satanium. He also provided instructions which were to be carried out to the last detail if things went wrong.

Cautiously, John Feather placed one drop of satanium on the professor's outstretched tongue.

Almost immediately the professor's eyes began to glow golden. His head swelled up to three times its normal size!

"You drivelling idiot!" he screamed at John Feather. "What are you looking at? A piece of wormflesh like you has no right to come into my presence without being requested!"

"But Professor," John Feather said. "You were the one who asked me to... "

"Get out of here you snivelling imbecile!" Professor Gribb screamed. "Before I tear you apart for having blue eyes! Blue-eyed dimwits should all be exterminated from the world!"

John Feather backed away from the professor and hid behind a metal cupboard.

Professor Gribb raised his arms until they were stretched out in front of him, and from the fingers of each hand blue bolts of electric energy flashed across the room, reducing the cupboard instantly to a pile of smouldering metal.

John Feather hurried out of the laboratory, through the front door and off down the steep road.

Professor Gribb followed. But his attention was drawn to other things which appeared to annoy him intensely.

"I've told them for years that no cars should be parked on this street!"

He raised his arms and several blue flashes later there was a neat row of ash-piles where each of the cars had once stood.

He continued to walk down the street. Well,

actually he didn't walk. It was too fast to be called 'walking'. In fact it was too fast to be called 'running'. It was an almost instantaneous movement from one place to another. No sooner had he thought where he'd like to be than he was there.

Halfway to the city centre, he noticed that a travelling funfair had been set up in the park. He came to a screeching halt.

"What an eyesore!" he ranted. "I must stop people having fun!"

He rushed into the funfair and within a few seconds the Big Wheel, the Octopus and the Dodgem cars were nothing but smouldering remains.

Once he reached the city centre, Professor Gribb wreaked havoc. Within the space of a few hours, he had flattened the Post Office Tower, destroyed the Palace and demolished the Parliament Buildings.

By evening the city was declared a disaster zone. The police had received reports of a man single-handedly destroying cars and buildings, but they failed to catch sight of him. Professor Gribb's speed of movement made him almost invisible as he sped from place to place.

At midnight he returned home. The satanium was beginning to wear off and he felt awful. He was terribly tired with a splitting headache.

On an impulse, he barged into his daughter's room. There she was, the poor bald thing, sleeping innocently.

Professor Gribb stretched out his hands and caressed her bald head.

"I'm so sorry," he said. "May all your hair grow back!"

A blue flash of electricity passed from his hands to his daughter's head. It had an immediate effect. Little wormlike creatures began to grow in all directions from her scalp. Longer and longer they grew, until sweet Kaylie had a flourishing headful of fingers!

"Oh dear!" Professor Gribb said. "What have I done now? I'm so sorry!"

He realised what he must do. He rushed into his laboratory. He had to destroy the apparatus he had used to make satanium. He raised his arms and, with a crackling flash of blue electricity, half of his laboratory was instantly reduced to ashes. It was his last act of power. He slumped to the floor and fell into a deep slumber.

In the morning he was roused by John Feather.

"Are you alright?" he asked timidly, afraid that the professor was still keen on destroying blue-eyed people.

Professor Gribb opened one eye.

"Is that you, Mr F... f... ?" he asked weakly. It seemed he couldn't remember Mr Feather's name.

The professor looked a sorry sight. His hair was as white as a swan's feathers. His head had somewhat reduced in size but was still twice as large as it had been originally. His eyes were still tinged with gold but they were also criss-crossed with red veins. His skin was ashen grey. He was unable to think clearly about anything. His mind could no longer concentrate on any one topic for longer than eight seconds. In short, the intense energy of the satanium had frizzled Professor Gribb's body and mind.

Mr Feather insisted that the professor eat something. Then he helped the professor to wash and shave himself.

Next, Mr Feather began to tidy up the laboratory.

"What a mess!" he exclaimed.

"Yes it is, Mr F... f... " Professor Gribb said. "I'm sorry about that."

John Feather swept up the ashes, but among them he found the test-tube containing the satanium.

"Look at this, Professor! The satanium wasn't destroyed. Perhaps it's indestructible!"

Professor Gribb looked sadly at the test-tube.

But he looked sadder still when little Kaylie came running into the laboratory.

"Daddy! Daddy!" she screamed. "Look what happened to me last night!"

John Feather backed off in horror when he saw the girl's headful of wriggling fingers.

"I still love you, K... k... k... " Barnaby said soothingly, though he could no longer remember his daughter's name.

"We must get rid of this stuff immediately," John Feather said.

"Yes," the professor agreed. "It must be sealed in concrete and thrown deep in... "

But the professor didn't finish his sentence. His attention had already turned elsewhere.

That same afternoon John Feather mixed up some concrete and encased the test-tube in it. The following day, when the concrete lump had dried, he drove up to Delvish Cave. The entrance had once been boarded up to prevent access, but now many of the wooden slats were missing. John Feather squeezed through into the darkness. With a torch, he wound his way cautiously into the dank stomach of the earth. Sleeping bats clung to the roof of the cavern in vast numbers, but they remained motionless, even when John Feather lost his footing and stumbled. He just managed to avoid falling over the edge of what seemed like a pit. He shone the beam down, but the light merely faded in its bottomless depths. He found a small pebble and threw it in. After what seemed like ages, he heard a small splash.

"This will do just fine," John Feather said.

"Good riddance!" he shouted, as he hurled the concrete lump containing the satanium into the pit.

"Good riddance!" he heard, echoing around the cave.

He listened carefully. Yes, that was it. A tiny splash. The satanium was truly buried now where it could no harm.

How wrong John Feather was!

Many years passed by. Kaylie grew up into a lovely young lady, though she always wore a hat or beret to conceal her headful of fingers. The loyal John Feather cared for Barnaby Gribb as best he could, never divulging to the world the extraordinary events he had witnessed. As for the professor, well, sadly he was never able to utter a complete sentence again. Periodically, though, he would mumble the words, "I'm sorry... " and a single tear would roll from each of his eyes. These tears were collected by John Feather using an eye-dropper and stored in a glass bottle on a shelf in the room that had once been the professor's laboratory. John Feather hoped one day to show the world that at least Professor Gribb was sorry for his actions.

This might have been the end of the story had it not been for the sighting of some extraordinary creatures. At first these were considered to be merely rumour. Someone reported having seen a fox with two tails. Another person claimed to have spotted a rabbit with three ears. Yet another discovered a crow which was unable to fly because it had been born wingless.

On investigation, it became apparent that these bizarre sightings were all occurring within a ten-mile radius of Delvish Cave. Photographs began to appear in the local newspapers: a pony with claws instead of hooves; a sheep with two heads; a pig with a beak instead of a snout. Then it was discovered that all the male fish in the river below the cave had suddenly turned female. And that an entire season's tadpoles had evolved into snails rather than frogs.

Some time later, Kaylie read about three children in a nearby suburb who had grown fingers from their heads instead of hair. Kaylie was shocked. This couldn't be a coincidence! So Kaylie began to research the problem. She felt there must be some connection between herself and the high incidence of physical abnormalities in the surrounding area.

She enrolled at the University to study astrobio-physicology. Like her father, she proved to be very, very, very, very intelligent. After she graduated, she persuaded John Feather to become her assistant.

"Mr Feather," she said. "I believe you know more about my father's work than you let on. I would like you to assist me in finding the cause of these physical aberrations. If we can establish the cause, we may be able to work on a cure."

"I can't," John Feather answered. "I spend all my time caring for your father. Besides that, I gave him my oath that I would never reveal the nature of his experiments."

A year later Professor Gribb's condition deteriorated and during the night he passed away quietly. At his funeral, scientists praised him for his early work and expressed their regret at his unfortunate demise. But none of them had any suspicion about his experiments with satanium and John Feather remained silent.

The day after the funeral, Kaylie once again begged John Feather to become her assistant.

"Please help me," she begged. "For my sake and for the sake of all those other poor children who are being afflicted."

"Alright," John Feather replied. "Now that I

don't have any more obligations towards your father."

Together, they began to restore the laboratory to its former glory. And John Feather revealed to Kaylie everything he knew about the production of satanium, about the professor's experiments during those fateful days, and of how he had disposed of the satanium deep within Delvish Cave.

"I am sure that the concrete casing around the satanium has cracked or disintegrated in some way," he explained to Kaylie. "The satanium is leaking out! It must be seeping into the water table below Delvish Cave and contaminating the streams."

"We must find an antidote," Kaylie said. "If only I knew the formulas my father used to produce satanium."

"I think I can help you with that," John Feather said, producing a pile of scorched notepaper from a locked cupboard. "These are what remains of Professor Gribb's notes."

Kaylie worked as hard as her father ever had, perhaps harder. She began her day at dawn, stopping only for breakfast, lunch and dinner – and of course tea-breaks at eleven o'clock in the morning, four o'clock in the afternoon, and nine o'clock at night. During these tea-breaks, she would sit in her father's old wicker chair and sip Earl Grey tea. All this time she searched for the formula that would save the city from the dreadful plague that her father had introduced all those years ago.

Day after day, year after year, Kaylie produced

and tested various compounds which might destroy
the power of satanium. Her laboratory filled with an
extraordinary collection of orchids, mushrooms and
rare berries from the forests of Borneo. The closer
she came to her goal, the more excited Kaylie
became.

One morning, during her tea-break, she exploded
with joy.

"My dear Feather!" she exclaimed. "I believe I
have done it! A substance that will render satanium
as harmless as mother's milk!"

During her afternoon tea-break, Kaylie worked
out most of the formula. During the evening tea-
break, she had almost solved the problem of how to
manufacture the product.

But there was still something lacking in her formula. As she sat in his old wicker chair late that
night, she felt uneasy.

"It needs an extra something," she said to herself
as she dozed off for a few moments. "Something
potent... "

"Perhaps I can help you," she heard a voice utter.

Kaylie sat up in a state of utter surprise! There,
on the end of her desk, wrapped in a mantle of
flames, perched a small fellow. His eyes were completely white, his ears resembled bat's wings. His
skin was scaly and his hands and feet were clawed
like a bird.

"Who are you?" Kaylie asked.

"Why, surely you recognise me?" the little fellow
said. "I've been your inspiration all these years.

The one who has given you all your best ideas."

"Rubbish!" Kaylie said. "I've never had anything to do with you!"

"Don't you dare speak to me like that, you vixen!" the demon screamed. "I know what your missing ingredient is, so you'd better listen to what I have to say."

"Get out of here!" Kaylie yelled.

The demon puffed up his chest in rage.

"I'll teach you a lesson you'll never forget!" he bellowed as he stepped towards Kaylie.

In self-defence, she reached for a bottle on the shelf nearest her. It happened to be the sorry bottle, filled to the brim with her father's tears.

As the demon lunged towards her, Kaylie threw the liquid all over the little fellow.

Boy, did he scream in agony! Those tears blistered his skin, then burned deep into his body, stripping his bones of all flesh, then dissolving the bones in a puff of smoke. His mouth let out a final scream before it disappeared altogether.

There was nothing left of the demon! No trace at all.

"Wow!" Kaylie exclaimed. "These tears are powerful! I wonder if they could be the missing ingredient?"

But when she examined the bottle, it was almost empty! Just a small pool of tears swished around in the bottom of the bottle. Nevertheless, she felt encouraged. She threw the tears in to a canister of boiling black syrup. It bubbled up in a golden froth.

Kaylie worked all night. It was still boiling in the morning when John Feather turned up for work.

"Mr Feather, I believe we have cause for celebration this morning."

Together they blended the antidote in the revolving tub which looked much like a washing machine. The liquid was passed through spiral tubes into thick-walled chambers where laser-beams flashed turquoise and yellow.

That very afternoon, the first drops of the antidote were finally distilled into a small test-tube. It was a victorious moment.

"Kaylie, you are a genius!" John Feather said.

"I only hope it works," Kaylie replied.

When enough antidote had been produced to fill the test-tube, Kaylie held it up to the light. The liquid was almost transparent, but tinged with gold.

"Beautiful!" she remarked.

She removed the beret from her head and gazed at herself in a small hand-mirror. She placed a single drop of the liquid on her scalp.

Almost immediately the fingers on her head began to shrink! Smaller and smaller, thinner and thinner, until they shrivelled away entirely.

"Wonderful, wonderful, wonderful!" John Feather exclaimed, clapping his hands and jumping up and down excitedly.

That same afternoon, Kaylie gave John Feather the test-tube containing what was left of the antidote. He drove up to Delvish Cave and squeezed through the boarded-up entrance into the darkness.

Carefully he wound his way into the stomach of the earth. Using his flashlight, he found his way to the pit where he had once hurled the concrete-wrapped satanium.

He held the test-tube of antidote in his hands for a moment.

"May this correct all the damage done in the past!" he said.

Then he cast the test-tube into the pit.

He listened carefully. Yes, that was it. A tiny splash.

There isn't much more to tell. Half of the female fish returned to being male. Tadpoles began to grow into frogs once again. Ponies were born with hooves instead of claws; sheep were born with one head, not two; pigs were born with snouts instead of beaks. Never again were two-tailed foxes sighted, nor three-eared rabbits, nor wingless crows. In time, all the fingers growing from children's heads shrank and then disappeared.

And what about Kaylie? Well, all I can tell you is that I bumped into her just the other week, and her head was covered with a gorgeous layer of golden hair.

Voice of Gloria Gale

The garden suburbs of Glitz City are where the rich folk live. Elegant cars cruise along opulent, tree-lined avenues before turning into long drives which lead to huge mansions. The gardens are all perfectly cared for and some have large ponds stocked with golden fish.

In one such mansion there lived a girl who had everything a person could wish for. Her name was Tyra. She lived with her mother and father and four older brothers.

Her parents were often away. Her father worked in the theatre and was always on tour somewhere or other. Her mother was a businesswoman with clients in every corner of the world. They made up for being away so much by bringing Tyra and her brothers expensive gifts from the countries they'd been visiting. Her brothers didn't seem to mind the arrangements – they had each other for company. But Tyra was alone much of the time, and missed her parents terribly.

The housekeeper tried her best to look after Tyra when the girl's parents were away. She made delicious meals for her three times a day. She put fresh flowers in Tyra's bedroom to cheer her up. And she often tried to talk to Tyra. But the girl barely responded to the housekeeper's efforts.

The huge house had once belonged to Tyra's aunt, who had been a top fashion model known as Gloria Gale. When she died, she had left the house to Tyra's mother.

There were albums in a cupboard containing countless photographs of Gloria Gale. Sometimes Tyra's mother showed them to her. The photographs were of a slender young lady with a pretty face wearing extraordinary clothes. Tyra thought her aunt was beautiful, though her mother usually commented on how skinny Gloria looked. Her aunt had been very famous and glamorous when she was alive. Pictures of her were used to advertise well-known perfumes and drinks.

Whenever Tyra's mother looked at the album, she wept.

"What a tragic waste!" she would say through her tears. "She was so young."

Tyra often wandered through the corridors and rooms of this house. In fact there were thrity-two rooms altogether, if you included the gym with its exercise machines, the indoor swimming pool and the photographic studio. Some rooms were seldom used, others never. There was one room, in particular, that Tyra was always afraid to enter. This was her aunt's bedroom, left the way it had been when she was still alive. There was a modern bed in the centre of the room and built-in wardrobes all round, with her aunt's fashionable garments still hanging inside them. But Tyra felt uncomfortable there, so she avoided it at all times.

One morning, Tyra awoke feeling quite ill. Her parents were both away in foreign countries. Her brothers had gone off to college. She looked in her mirror and saw the reflection of a girl who wasn't as pretty and slender as her famous aunt. Tyra decided she was too ill to go to school that day, so she stayed in bed until lunchtime. By mid-afternoon she was bored. She was even fed-up with the new electronic keyboard which her parents had given her when they'd last visited home.

Suddenly, she heard a distant voice calling.

"Tyra! Tyra! Don't be so glum and gloomy. Come up here, dear!"

It was a woman's voice. But who could it be? There was nobody else at home apart from her and the housekeeper, and it certainly wasn't the housekeeper.

Tyra was petrified, but there was something compelling in that voice, something hypnotic which forced her to jump out of bed, put on her dressing gown and walk out of her room into the passage.

She heard the voice again.

"Come up the stairs, sweetie! Do as I say!"

As if in a trance, Tyra obeyed.

"In here!" the voice said. It seemed to be coming from Gloria Gale's bedroom!

Tyra couldn't believe it. Her body trembled with fear.

"Don't be afraid, honey! Turn the handle!"

Tyra didn't want to enter that room, but there was a terrible sorcery in that voice which forced her to turn the handle on the bedroom door and step inside.

"Tyra! How you've grown!"

Tyra couldn't see anyone in the room. But the voice was louder now.

"We're having a party in here and you're invited!"

"Who's speaking to me?" Tyra whispered. "Where are you?"

"I'm here, sweetheart!" the voice said. "Come nearer!"

The voice seemed to be coming from the full-length mirror on the far side of the room. Tyra wanted to leave. She didn't want to go nearer. But there was a power in the voice which forced her feet to take steps across the room.

She looked in the mirror but couldn't see anything other than her own image.

Again she heard the voice. It seemed to issue from the mirror or from behind it.

"You can't come to the party in a dressing gown!"

the voice said. "Go put on one of those lovely dresses. Something white, I think."

Tyra didn't want to try on any of Gloria Gale's dresses, but the eerie voice compelled her to open one of the wardrobes. Within a short time, she changed into a stylish white silk dress, wrapped a fringed white scarf around her neck and slipped into a pair of white shoes.

Tyra examined herself in the full-length mirror. Her aunt's dress didn't fit perfectly, but she thought it looked quite glamorous. "How lovely!" the voice said.

"Where are you?" Tyra asked. "I can't see you!"

"Look carefully, dear!" the voice said.

It was then that Tyra noticed a small gap in the centre of the mirror, where a tiny fragment of the mirror glass had chipped away. The crack was only as broad as a pencil, but Tyra put her eye up against it and peeped through.

What a shock Tyra received! There, on the other side of the mirror, in a huge room, was the owner of the evil voice!

Tyra recognised her immediately. It was none other than Gloria Gale! Her aunt was standing there looking straight back at Tyra, her eyes with dark rings around them, as if they'd been painted with charcoal, and her cheeks so pale they seemed to be dusted with chalk.

Behind Gloria were hundreds of guests, all slim and dressed in the latest fashions. They were having a good time, it seemed. Some were dancing to disco music, others were chatting among themselves and laughing. Still others were preening themselves in front of oval mirrors.

Tyra was so frightened, she stood fixed to the floor.

"Come join us!" Gloria urged Tyra, beckoning with her finger.

"How?" Tyra asked.

"Just climb through the crack, honey!"

Tyra didn't want to, but her aunt's voice was too powerful for her. Tyra had to try. But how was it possible? The crack was so narrow. Not even her baby finger would fit through that tiny gap.

"Oh, you silly goose!" Gloria said. "You're much too plump! You'll never fit through!"

Tyra didn't like being insulted. Tears formed in her eyes.

Gloria Gale's voice boomed out at her.

"In future you're to eat nothing that's white!"

"What do you mean?" Tyra asked.

"You must not eat food that has any white ingredient in it! Now go away at once!"

The voice of her aunt rang out its evil spell. Tyra felt a dreadful pain rush through her body as she realised she had no choice but to do as she'd been told.

The housekeeper wasn't pleased.

"Oh, heaven help us! What's come over you? Nothing white? No bread? No cakes?"

But Tyra insisted and that was that. From now on the housekeeper had to make meals and snacks without rice or flour or sugar or milk or salt.

It was difficult for Tyra to miss out on so many of her favourite foods, but she couldn't help herself.

After a month, Tyra had lost a quarter of her weight.

Then one afternoon, to her horror, she heard that terrible voice again. She knew it was Gloria Gale calling to her. She had to obey.

Up she went again to her aunt's bedroom.

"Put on one of those lovely dresses!" the voice suggested. "Something red."

The voice was irresistible. Tyra changed into a red silk dress, wrapped a red fringed scarf around her neck and slipped into a pair of red shoes.

Tyra examined herself in the full-length mirror. Her aunt's dress still didn't fit properly. Her face looked sallow now that her cheeks had lost some of their colour and shape.

"How lovely!" the voice said. "Come and join us!"

Tyra felt she had no choice except to obey. But how could she? Not even her baby finger would fit through that tiny gap.

"You're still too plump, you silly goose!" Gloria Gale said. "In future, not only will you avoid white foods, but you will also eat nothing red. Is that clear?"

Tyra felt sick when she heard this! But the spell was so powerful! Tyra knew that she would have to do as she'd been told.

The housekeeper was extremely upset.

"Heavens above! Whatever next? Nothing red? No ketchup? No bacon?"

But Tyra seemed to have made up her mind, so the housekeeper prepared meals without meat, tomatoes, cherries, plums or strawberries.

Again it was painful for Tyra to miss out on so many delicious foods, but she couldn't help herself.

After a month, Tyra had lost half her weight.

Then one afternoon, to her dismay, she heard Gloria Gale calling to her again. The evil voice had to be obeyed.

Up she went to her aunt's bedroom. This time the voice demanded that she dress in yellow. Tyra changed into a yellow silk dress, wrapped a yellow fringed scarf around her neck and slipped into a pair of yellow shoes.

She examined herself in the mirror. Her aunt's dress still didn't fit perfectly, and she was quite startled by her own pale and sickly image.

But the voice said, "How lovely! You're looking better and better! Do come and join us!"

As if in a bad dream, Tyra had to obey. Yet, how could she? Not even her baby finger would fit through that tiny gap.

"You're still too plump, you silly goose!" Gloria Gale said. "In future, not only will you avoid red and white foods, but you will also eat nothing yellow!"

Tyra felt so weak, she almost fainted, but her aunt's magical voice wouldn't release its grip on her. Tyra was forced to do as she'd been told.

The housekeeper was distressed.

"Lord have mercy, child! You're wasting away! Nothing yellow? No custard? No omelettes?"

But Tyra stuck to what the voice told her to do. The housekeeper had to find recipes without cheese, butter, eggs, lemons or sweet corn.

Tyra hated the food she was presented with. It barely had any taste. But she couldn't help herself.

After a month, Tyra had lost three-quarters of her weight.

Then one afternoon – oh no! – she heard Gloria Gale calling to her again. As if she were sleepwalking, Tyra obeyed.

Up she went again to her aunt's bedroom. This time the voice commanded her to dress in green. Tyra changed into a green silk dress, wrapped a green fringed scarf around her neck and slipped into a pair of green shoes.

She examined herself in the mirror. She barely recognised her image, with its hollow eyes and sunken cheeks, wearing a dress that almost fitted, but not quite.

"How lovely!" the evil voice said. "You're looking elegant! Now come and join us!"

Tyra didn't want to, but the magic in that terrible voice forced her to try and climb through the crack in the mirror.

Yet how could she? Not even her baby finger would fit through that tiny gap.

"You're still too plump, you silly goose!" Gloria Gale said. "In future, not only will you avoid yellow, red and white foods, but you will also eat nothing green!"

Tyra was shocked. How would she survive? But the evil voice of her aunt had to be obeyed.

The housekeeper was beside herself with worry.

"What the devil's wrong with you, child? What will your parents say? They'll think it's all my fault. Nothing green? No vegetables? No salads?"

But Tyra insisted. The housekeeper despaired.

"You poor waif! If you don't eat lettuce or peas or broccoli or celery or cucumber, what on earth will you eat?"

It soon became clear. Tyra didn't eat anything at all! She drank only pure water, which was transparent and had no colour.

It was torment to eat nothing. She longed for the delicious foods that the housekeeper used to cook.

After a month she weighed almost nothing at all.

Then one awful afternoon, Tyra heard the terrible voice that she hoped she would never hear again. There was no resisting it. She had to obey.

Up she went to her aunt's bedroom. This time the voice instructed her to dress in black. Tyra changed into a black silk dress, wrapped a black fringed scarf around her neck and slipped into a pair of black shoes.

She examined herself in the mirror. This time her aunt's dress fitted perfectly! But the girl she saw in the mirror looked so wasted and sad!

Despite this, the voice said, "How lovely! You look fabulous! Come and join us!"

Tyra burst out weeping, but her aunt's voice was powerful.

"Climb through the crack!" it shrieked.

Tyra approached the mirror. And this time her baby finger fitted through the tiny gap! She was terrified! Surely the rest of her wouldn't fit through?

Just as she wondering about this, she felt her baby finger gripped from the other side of the mirror. Gloria Gale was tugging on her finger, heaving and pulling her through the crack. Tyra struggled desperately to stay on this side of the mirror.

"Come through, sweetheart!" Gloria intoned, as she tugged on Tyra's finger.

Oh, that voice! That terrible, terrible voice! Its powerful, evil magic sapped Tyra of her strength. She was losing the struggle!

Suddenly, with a lot of squeezing and pain – plop! – she fell through to the other side.

"I'm so glad you've come to join us," Gloria Gale said. "My, you do look gorgeous!"

Tyra was now able to see her aunt close-up – the famous Gloria Gale, slim and pretty, just as she appeared in all the photographs. But there was something so frightening about her! She looked like nothing but skin and bone to Tyra – her cheeks pale and sunken, her eyes hollow and glazed.

In fact, Gloria Gale was so thin and weightless, she cast no shadow on the floor, despite the light blazing down on her from the crystal chandelier above. A cold chill passed through Tyra's body. She turned to examine the other guests and soon realised that not one person in the room was casting a shadow!

Oh no! What about herself? She looked down at the ground in front of her feet. No sign of a shadow! She looked to the left, to the right, and behind her. No shadow at all!

"There are so many people I'd like you to meet," Gloria Gale said, introducing Tyra first to one person, then another.

Many young men came to say "Hello" to Tyra and she was polite to them all. But how cold their hands were! Cold as corpses. And how pale their faces! Except for the dark rings around their eyes.

The chattering and laughing continued endlessly. Conversations about nothing in particular, jokes which weren't really funny, although people laughed as if they were. Every so often one of the guests would comb their hair in front of one of the many mirrors in the room, or would disappear for a few moments, only to return in a new outfit, keeping up with the latest fashions.

The longer Tyra was there, the more she lost track of time, until she barely knew if hours were passing, or days, or months, or even years. One moment was exactly like the next and nothing ever changed, except for the clothes.

It occurred to Tyra that she was trapped in a world where nothing and nobody was real. If only she could escape from this endless party! But every door led only to a changing-room. There was no way out!

In the meantime, Tyra's mother and father returned from abroad. The housekeeper had contacted them urgently, sobbing with anguish as she told them that Tyra had vanished. She had searched the house but found only discarded clothes.

Tyra's parents were overcome with grief and remorse. They contacted the police, but they also could find no trace of Tyra.

"It's all our fault!" Tyra's mother wept. "We didn't take good care of her."

"We should never have left her on her own so much," her father wailed. "Perhaps we'll never see our daughter again."

"Oh no, don't say that," her mother said, sobbing.

Tyra's four brothers were also upset.

"We should have kept an eye on her," they admitted. "Now we must go out into the world and search for her."

They left the rich suburb in Glitz City and journeyed for one year and a day in search of their sister. North, south, east and west they each went, but there was no sign of Tyra anywhere! However, on their travels, each of the brothers married and their four young brides were brought back to live in the enormous house.

The wives got on well together. They spent a lot of time in each other's company, singing each other's songs and learning from each other about life in the four corners of the world. Although it was a sad house to live in, the four wives kept themselves jolly and in good spirits.

Now it happened that one day they were exploring the large house when they heard a voice calling from upstairs.

"Come up here, my dears!"

The four wives were astonished. But there was something compelling in the voice which forced them to go upstairs.

The voice was coming from Gloria Gale's bedroom!

"In here, my honeys!" the voice said.

The four wives shook with fear.

"Don't be afraid, sweeties, we're having a party and you're all invited!"

The four ladies didn't want to enter that room, but some terrible power in the voice forced them to turn the handle on the bedroom door and step inside.

"Come join the party!" the voice called from behind the full-length mirror.

The four wives hesitated, but the evil voice forced them to walk across the room.

"Oh, you can't come to the party in those old dresses!" the voice said. "Go and find yourself some lovely dresses in that wardrobe."

The four ladies felt there was something very odd going on, but the hypnotic voice persuaded them to open the wardrobe and dress in four glamorous outfits which didn't even fit properly.

"How lovely you all look," the voice said. "Now, come on through!"

"Through where?" they asked.

"Through the crack in the mirror!" the voice commanded.

The four ladies each put their eye to the crack,

one after another, and peeped through. There, on the other side, was the owner of the evil voice – Gloria Gale, with her hollow eyes and sunken cheeks – beckoning with her finger for them to come through the mirror.

"Through this small gap!" they laughed. "You must be joking! We couldn't fit through there."

"That's because you're all too plump, you silly geese!" the voice said.

The lady from the north, dressed in white, examined herself in the full-length mirror.

"You think I'm too plump, do you?" she said to Gloria Gale.

"Without a doubt! And in future," Gloria Gale commanded, "you're to eat nothing that's white! Do you understand?"

"What twaddle!" said the lady from the north. "I like myself just the way I am."

She threw off the white dress and put on her own clothes.

The lady from the south, dressed in red, examined herself in the mirror.

"You surely don't think I'm too plump?"

"You most certainly are!" the evil voice replied. "From now on you're to eat nothing that's red!"

"Absolute rot!" said the lady from the south. "I enjoy my food and I feel good."

She immediately discarded the red dress and put on her own clothes.

The lady from the east, dressed in yellow, examined herself in the mirror.

"It's not me that's plump! It's this dress that's so tight it would only fit a stick!"

"Of course it's not the dress, you fat-head!" fumed the evil voice. "In future you're to eat nothing that's yellow!"

"Absurd!" exclaimed the lady from the east. "You can't tell me what to do!"

She flung off the yellow dress and put on her own clothes.

The lady from the west, dressed in green, examined herself in the mirror.

"Plump, shmump! Who cares anyway?"

"I do!" the evil voice cried. "From now on you're to eat nothing that's green!"

"Stuff and nonsense!" said the lady from the west. "I don't want to end up looking deathly like you do!"

With that, she cast off the green dress and put on her own clothes.

Then the four ladies burst out laughing.

"We've never heard anything so ridiculous in all our lives."

They turned their back on the mirror and were about to leave the room when they heard a tiny voice squeaking, "Help! Help!"

They looked around to find a finger poking though the crack in the mirror.

"Please, help me! She's a witch! Pull me through!"

The lady from the north grabbed hold of the finger and began to pull. Then the lady from the south took hold of her. Likewise the lady from the east began to pull and finally the lady from the west.

But on the other side of the mirror, Gloria Gale had grabbed hold of Tyra and was holding her fiercely.

"Pull harder!" Tyra called.

All four women pulled and pulled, until with a great heave a young girl came squeezing through the crack and – plop! – she landed in the room with them.

"Thank you, thank you!" she said. "It was so awful in there!"

The voice of Gloria Gale came shrieking through the hole in the mirror.

"Don't think I'm finished with you!"

"Who are you?" the four women asked the young girl.

"I'm Tyra," the girl explained.

"Tyra! Our sister-in-law!" the four ladies rejoiced. "You've come back to us! Hooray!"

They hugged Tyra and danced around the room with her. Tyra didn't even notice that her shadow had returned and was dancing around the room beneath her feet.

"You poor thing," said the lady from the north. "You're so frail."

"You're nothing but skin and bone," said the lady from the south.

"You look like you haven't had a good meal for months," said the lady from the east.

"We'll help you to get well again," said the lady from the west.

When Tyra had changed out of the black dress into her own clothes, they took her downstairs.

What a rejoicing there was when Tyra's mother and father and brothers saw her again!

The housekeeper was beside herself with happiness. "Oh, thank goodness! What a relief! Please can I cook with colours again?" she asked.

"Yes, let's have something to eat right now to celebrate!" Tyra's mother suggested.

The housekeeper laid the table and the family sat down.

A plate of food was placed in front of Tyra. But just as she was about to lift some to her mouth, she heard a voice calling down to her from her aunt's bedroom.

"You're too plump, you silly goose! You shouldn't eat anything!"

Tyra hesitated. She put the food back on the plate.

"I don't want to be like my aunt," Tyra exclaimed. "What can I do?"

"Just start with a little of each colour!" her mother suggested.

Tyra lifted the food to her mouth. The four wives smiled and cheered as Tyra nibbled snacks that were white, red, yellow and green.

"My darling daughter!" her mother said, wrapping her arms around her.

Path

On a day much like any day, a father much like any father and a daughter much like any daughter went out for a walk. The daughter's name was Nayette.

They lived on the edge of the city, so the countryside was within easy reach. Through the park they walked, around the supermarket, over the railway bridge, across the farm, and there they were, beyond the sprawling suburbs of the city.

They were ascending the gentle rise through the pastures where sheep were grazing when a tall, red-bearded fellow with a rucksack and stick came striding towards them.

"Good day to you," he greeted them amiably.

"And to you too," Nayette's father answered.

"Oh, are you in for a surprise today!" the fellow

said. "If you take the path from Abbick that leads across the hills to Zander you will be amazed."

"We weren't intending to go that far," Nayette's father said.

"Oh, you should, you should," the tall fellow enthused. "The place is magical."

"Let's go there, Daddy," Nayette pleaded.

"Okay sweetheart," her father replied.

The red-bearded fellow smiled and passed by. He went the way they had come, across the farm, over the railway bridge, around the supermarket, through the park to the city.

They went the way he had come, following the steep path up towards Zander.

When they reached the crest of the first ridge, they gazed back at the city. Somewhere among that sea of roofs was their own house.

That thought disturbed Nayette's father.

"Oh no!" he exclaimed to himself. "I left the front door of the house unlocked!"

For a moment he considered turning back. But then he calculated that by this time they were so far from home that it was almost as well continue to Zander. From there they could hire a taxi-cab to take them home.

So as not to trouble his daughter, he kept these thoughts to himself. But how uncomfortable he felt! In his mind's eye, he could easily see that with the door of the house unlocked, a burglar would get in. With no one else in the house, the burglar would have plenty of time to rummage through all the

drawers and cupboards of the house and steal whatever he wanted.

While her father was absorbed in these imagin-
ings, a glint of golden light caught Nayette's eye.
She turned to see what it was. There, a little way off
in a field, was a bird of uncanny beauty, the feathers
of its wings glinting gold in the sunlight. Nayette
knew immediately what it was – a jula-bird. Her
mother had once told her about jula-birds – how
extraordinary they were, but how rare to find.

Nayette stared and stared as the bird pecked
around in the long grass. It was only then that she
noticed a similar bird a short distance away from the
first. As she focused her gaze on the second bird,
she noticed a third, and a fourth, and a fifth. In fact,
the long grass was teeming with jula-birds. How had
she failed to notice them until now? There were so
many of them, gleaming golden as they strutted
here and there.

Then, almost as if one of them had given a command, they all rose softly into the air. What a magnificent sight! The whole flock moved in harmony,
as if they were a single creature, first flying one way
and then the other, rising all the while into the blue
sky. As they swung to the left, their wings shone
golden, and as they swung to the right, silver!

Nayette had to shield her eyes from their brightness. It was as if she were gazing into an ocean
reflecting the sun's rays. She was certain she had
never before seen birds quite so beautiful.

They flew off into the distance, dancing in formation across the sky, and then with one last golden glint they disappeared behind the next hill and were gone from sight.

Nayette walked on quietly beside her father. He was anxiously scratching the top of his head, as if to encourage his brain to remember whether he had locked the front door or not.

"How stupid of me!" he thought.

That burglar would be in the house by now, going through all the rooms. He pictured the burglar stealing all their clothes and the camera he kept on the top shelf of his wardrobe. It was quite a new camera and had cost a great deal, even though he'd bought it on a sale. Probably the burglar would remove all his most treasured possessions and load them into a van – his music player, his piano, his TV system, his computers. Everything!

Nayette and her father walked on over the high ridge and arrived at a small sheltered valley which lay bathed in sunlight.

"It's lovely here, isn't it?" Nayette said to her dad.

"Yes, darling," her dad responded, taking hold of her hand. He scanned the scenery for a moment, but soon became absorbed in his thoughts again.

In the centre of the valley, just ahead of them, was an imposing tree.

Nayette released her hand from her father's and ran towards the tree. She walked all the way around it, gasping with astonishment. The branches were resplendent with buds, each the size of a plum and in appearance just like a flame – red and orange and yellow. Nayette stared and stared. To her astonishment, right in front of her very eyes, one of the buds began to unfold. Slowly, perfectly, it unwrapped its glossy petals, stretching them gracefully, like a fist opening its fingers. From the centre of the bloom an exquisite scent wafted to Nayette's nostrils, a scent sweeter and more delicate than any perfume in any shop in the whole wide world. Almost immediately a delicate butterfly started probing the flower with its long tongue, sucking out the delicious nectar within.

When the butterfly was done, the flower began to pale. The colours faded from its petals and within seconds shrivelled and fell to the ground.

Nayette was shocked to discover how short-lived the beauty of the flower was. She had hoped it might last forever. But then, as suddenly as the first flower had bloomed, a second one now began to unfold its petals. Nayette was enchanted! Another butterfly arrived, sucked at the nectar within the flower, and again the petals faded and dropped to the ground.

Almost immediately a third began to flower. Slowly its petals opened. The tree, she thought, was like a firework in slow motion, shooting out its colourful rockets, which then faded one by one and fell to the ground.

Nayette was filled with wonder and was certain she had never before set eyes upon a tree quite so beautiful.

"Come on, Nayette!" she heard her father call. "We can't dawdle on the way."

Nayette was reluctant to leave the Firework Tree, but she knew she had to. She joined her father again on the path. He was fishing around in his anorak pockets, searching for something. His car keys! He couldn't find them.

"Blast!" he thought.

If the burglar got into the house, then he'd probably find the keys in his desk and steal the car, his pride and joy. Not only that, he thought, but if the burglar rummaged through his desk, he'd find bank cards and be able to withdraw all their savings. Nayette's father was consumed with misery, but said nothing of all this to his daughter, not wishing to upset her.

They walked on together, Nayette and her father, until they entered the gorge. Tall rock cliffs rose on either side of them. Nayette thought she heard something. She stopped for a moment to listen. Her father paced on ahead. She could hear a sort of whispering, singing sound.

She stepped forward again and followed the twists and turns which the path took through the gorge. The whispered singing was getting nearer.

As she turned the next bend, a tremendous noise like a great symphony orchestra regaled her ears. Before her was an enormous waterfall! So high was the cliff over which it plunged that it seemed to be dropping from the sky itself. Nayette looked up and saw small rainbows playing in the mists sprayed out from the falling waters.

She was riveted to the spot. She stared and stared. Never had she experienced anything like this before! Or heard anything quite so magnificent! Wherever the tumbling water struck a rock, it uttered a ringing sound. And all the water together combined to produce the most majestic music, swirling with different themes, sometimes booming and deep, at other times, tinkling like miniature bells.

"Nayette, are you coming or are you going to stand there forever?"

It was her father, shouting to make his voice heard over the music of the falls.

"It's getting late," he said.

Nayette wished she could spend forever listening to the waterfall music. She was certain she had never before heard any music quite so beautiful.

Nayette's father suggested she walk quickly now up the damp, stone steps. He wanted to get home as soon as possible. It would probably be too late anyway. The burglar would have already stolen everything. Nayette's father could see it all in his mind: the family would descend into poverty again. Without money or a car he would probably lose his job. He would have to sell the house in order to survive with Nayette. He would be forced to live in rented accommodation. Would he even be able to provide Nayette with enough food to eat?

The steps carved in the rock were slippery and steep. They led up from the waterfall to the summit of Zander Point. Up and up the steps wound, eventually broadening out onto a high plateau overlooking the countryside below. Tall columns of rock stood around them like giant guards.

Nayette breathed deeply of the air and took in the splendid view. As she did so, she suddenly spotted a white animal grazing on the slopes behind some young fir trees. The animal shied away as her father stomped past.

But Nayette longed to see the creature again. She slowed down and, as if she were wearing velvet slippers, softly tip-toed off the path towards the fir trees. Then she stood dead-still, holding her breath, her eyes as wide as egg-cups.

She watched and waited. After a while, a small white hoof stepped into view from behind a tree. This was followed by what appeared to be a small white gazelle, with beautiful, gentle eyes.

Nayette stared and stared. She could scarcely believe what she was seeing – a young gazelle with a single horn in the middle of its forehead!

It looked up at Nayette. She thought the creature might flee when it saw a human being. But it didn't. Instead it took another step forward, and another, approaching ever closer to Nayette.

Eventually, it reached her. Nayette didn't move a muscle. The creature lowered its head. Slowly and deliberately it touched Nayette's arm with its elegant, spiral-patterned horn.

It was an amazing feeling. Nayette's arm glowed with a warmth which spread up to her shoulders then radiated across into her whole body. Her heart nearly burst with pleasure.

"I told you we need to hurry!" Nayette's father shouted irritably, coming back up the path to fetch her.

Instantly, the unicorn gazelle bounded off into the darkness of the forest.

Tears fell from Nayette's eyes. Her father had scared off the wonderful creature.

But still, she was so grateful for seeing it. She was certain she had never before seen an animal quite so beautiful. Its touch had changed her forever. She knew something magical had happened! As if, in that single moment, the creature had chosen her to be the recipient of its love.

Nayette's father fumed on the way down the mountainside. He was not only concerned about how long the walk had taken, but he was distraught by what he knew would happen to his daughter if all their wealth had been stolen by the burglar. He clearly saw that Nayette would have to walk around in ragged clothing and that social workers would come to take her away from him. He was almost weeping by the time he and Nayette descended into Zander.

On the outskirts of the little village, a man came striding towards them. It was the tall red-bearded fellow with rucksack and stick they had seen before.

"Did you have a good time?" he asked.

"Oh yes," Nayette said. "The path was magical."

"Was it?" her father asked.

"Yes," Nayette said. "We saw the golden Jula-birds and the Firework Tree. We heard the Waterfall Music and best of all was the Unicorn Gazelle. It even touched me with its horn."

"We saw nothing of the sort," Nayette's father said. "Don't make up such nonsense."

"I'm not!" Nayette insisted.

"Anyway, we have to be on our way," Nayette's father said, "because I have important business to get back to."

Nayette said goodbye to the bearded fellow.

"Thanks for telling us to take that path," she said gratefully.

Nayette's father took hold of Nayette's hand and led her hastily down the path.

But suddenly he stopped.

"How terrible!" he exclaimed. "I've just under-stood!"

"What?" Nayette asked.

"Don't you see?" he said. "That man's the burglar."

"Which man?"

"That red-bearded fellow who told us to take the path from Abbick to Zander!"

"Of course he isn't," Nayette said.

"Don't you see?" her father explained. "He specially told us to take that path so that he would have the time to go to our house and steal all our belongings."

"He didn't!" Nayette said. "He's a lovely man."

"You'll see," Nayette's father said. "Let's hurry!"

They made their way down into Zander where Nayette's father hired a taxi which he ordered to zoom back towards their house.

"Faster, faster!" he ordered the taxi-driver.

Eventually they arrived home. Nayette's father paid the taxi-driver, then rushed to his front door.

It was locked. He hadn't left it unlocked after all. And no burglar had come, nor had anything been stolen.

"I'm sorry I thought badly of the red-bearded fellow," Nayette's father said, hugging his daughter. "Do you think one day we could try walking the path again?"

Mirror, Mirror

A *child* in the mirror sees a beast,
a beast in the mirror sees an outcast,
an outcast in the mirror sees a rebel.

A *rebel* in the mirror sees a coward,
a coward in the mirror sees a soldier,
a soldier in the mirror sees a captive.

A *captive* in the mirror sees a bride,
a bride in the mirror sees a gambler,
a gambler in the mirror sees a hero.

A *hero* in the mirror sees a child.